TEARS

ON A SUNDAY

AFTERNOON

MICHAEL PRESLEY

BESTSELLING AUTHOR OF *BLACKFUNK*

TEARS
ON A SUNDAY
AFTERNOON

SBI

STREBOR BOOKS

NEW YORK LONDON TORONTO SYDNEY

Strebor Books
P.O. Box 6505
Largo, MD 20792

ISBN-13 978-0-7394-8063-2

Cover design: © www.mariondesigns.com

Manufactured in the United States of America

DEDICATION

To my mom and my daughter, Meekaya.

PROLOGUE

Ian's fist slammed into my ribs, making a crackling sound as my rib bones were shattered. I held my fists over my forehead to protect my face from Al's fist, which had found its mark on the right side of my head. I was no boxer, but I knew the basics as I doubled over in pain on my way to the ground. Larry's twelve-inch, red and white Air Jordans found my stomach, lifting me off the ground with the force of a hurricane. Gravity and agony pitched me back down; I was a painful, bloody mess.

"Donald Watson, you pretty motherfucker. You think you can fuck any woman you want? Aisha's my girl. I'm going to kill you for fucking her." Ian's fist drove me deeper into the concrete foundation of our high school.

"Somebody call security! They're going to kill him!" I heard a female voice scream.

Al surprised me with a left punch, leaving my mouth filled with blood.

"Let's stab the motherfucker," Larry said.

I was staring at about twenty different feet, all different sizes and shapes. I couldn't lift my head high enough to see their faces.

"Naw, I want this motherfucker to suffer. I want his dick to go soft every time he tries to fuck," Ian responded.

Pain created a small blanket of darkness as someone's shoes dug into my back.

"I say let's kill the motherfucker, Ian. He fucked your girl on the steps during third period. Look around; the entire school knows about this shit." Larry had this deceptive, whiny voice. At six feet five inches and close to two hundred and eighty pounds, his grip on my neck prevented the slight amount of oxygen that was left in my system from circulating.

"Give me the knife, Larry. I'm going to cut this motherfucker's balls off."

My body was about to shut down as my pants were being pulled from under me.

"Donald, you've got to pray to God for help," my grandmother's voice rang out in my head.

I prayed like I never had before as I lay on the cold ground; about to lose my manhood.

"Al, hold down his leg," Ian demanded.

"Somebody stop them! They're out of control!" an unknown boy's voice shouted.

"You stop them! They've got knives and guns." another voice answered.

With the last bit of senses in my body quickly fading, I felt the knife dig into my scrotum. My eyes fluttered to Grandma's God, asking Him for help.

"They're cutting his balls off! Somebody do something!" a young girl screamed.

Her voice was my last recollection as I woke up in St. Mary's. I was hospitalized for three weeks and on bed rest for another six. I learned that Ian and his friends were doing a stint in Juvie when I returned to school. Aisha tried to get with me again, but I wouldn't go for it. Her pussy wasn't worth it and quite honestly, I had bigger fish to fry. Within the following three months, I fucked Al's sister, Ian's sister and Larry's mother, who was fine for her age. What? Did you think I would stop fucking? Michael Jordan plays basketball like I play women. Getting pussy is the only damn thing I do well. Unlike him, I won't embarrass myself and try to do anything else.

CHAPTER 1
TWENTY YEARS LATER

I was pushed through the revolving exit door of the office building by two ladies rushing to leave. They stared at me as if I had interrupted their flight into the streets. I smiled, knowing that I could make them walk right back into the building and forget about the kids and the husbands at home. Another day, I would have done exactly that, but today I already had plans. As I walked through the corridor, I was constantly bumped by hordes of people heading to the revolving doors. I glanced at my gold Movado; it was ten after five. I navigated to the line of elevators that carried the workers up and down every day. I stepped aside as more than a dozen business people in suits pushed out of one of them. I had been in the building earlier to set up a project with a group of engineers from our office. It was an extensive project that would require long, tedious hours. It was similar to one we had done on Staten Island a few weeks ago. During that visit, I had met one of the secretaries, Donna August, who had been with the company for five years. Brian Louis, a tall, dark coworker from Brooklyn, had made the introduction. He had spent at least forty-five minutes of the first hour trying to talk to Donna. I paid very little attention to them. Brian was single and the world was his oyster. Marriage somewhat limits the playing field so I had to take a different path with women, a path that denoted understanding. Admitting being married to women who interested me didn't make a damn difference in determining whether or not we fucked. My pretty face was all they needed to see and it was on.

Brian and I had eaten lunch together almost every day since I had come on board at Reason Consulting, the largest black engineering firm in New York. Engineers at Reason were not hired based on their résumés, but from recommendations by one of the company's board members. My father-in-law had gotten me employment within a few months after the wedding. Over lunch at Au Bon Pain, Brian told me that Donna was dripping for me. She was "dripping for me" after a brief hello but this was not extraordinary. Numerous women had yanked off their panties the first time I had ever walked into their apartments. That's the life of a pretty boy.

Brian was cool. There wasn't a jealous bone in his body. He had been feeling her but she was feeling only me. She jumped up and shook my hand after I walked into her office and over to her desk. I must tell you that I was very impressed. She was around five-nine with a dark complexion and a body almost any man would crawl on his knees after. Almost any man, but not me; I don't get down like that. I had fucked women that men would have killed themselves over. During our conversation, she told me to hold on. She needed to file an important document. When she turned around, she was a black man's butter; all a man wanted to do was spread it.

I showed the security guard my temporary ID to gain easy access back into the building. I had left the building at 2:00 P.M. to go and pick up my son, Emerald, from school. I didn't have to do that, but whenever I got a break at work, I tried to spend as much time with him as possible. My grandmother and my son were my only true loves.

I stepped into the empty elevator and pressed the button for the 25th floor; anxious to pick up where we had left off.

It was approximately five-fifteen when I knocked on the office door. Donna opened the door, led me to a couch in front of her desk, and asked me to wait. A few minutes passed and a man I hadn't seen before came in and spoke to her briefly. He had a large Kenneth Cole briefcase in his right hand and, upon further inspection, I noticed a gold handcuff was keeping the briefcase in place. Then he left.

"I'm so wound up," Donna said as she slumped down in her chair.

"That's work. Five days a week, two days to think about it, then five days back at work," I replied.

"You're very beautiful," she said with an edge of seduction in her voice.

That comment had gotten me into and out of trouble from the time I was old enough to remember. Sometimes it seemed like I could get away with murder. My looks were the result of a crime perpetrated on my mother when she was incarcerated at the Delvin Correctional Facility in upstate New York. Three white corrections officers had raped her. My mother took her own life shortly after my birth.

"I know," I said, smiling. "But thanks for the compliment anyway."

"You're mixed, aren't you?" she asked. "With that curly hair and those blue eyes, you've got to be."

"Yeah, my father was white and my mother was a Southern girl."

"So, who did you inherit that six-foot slender frame from? Your mother or father?"

"I don't know." I was being honest. Since nobody had wanted to set up DNA tests for three white men, his identity had remained a mystery.

Donna stood and walked to the front of the desk. "Come over here. Let me see how much taller you are than me."

It was a bullshit line, but the games had begun. I would not have been there unless I was willing to play.

I stood in front of her, with her hard nipples pushing against my shirt. Her skin smelled like fresh-picked apricots. She looked up at me, her luscious red lips glistening against the dark pigmentation of her face.

"I…"

It was all she got out of her mouth as my lips joined hers. She should have slapped me then. Maybe I should have slapped myself for making such assumptions, but neither of us did. Instead, her mouth feasted on mine as my hand went to the front of her blouse. The snaps came apart, like dry-rotted steel wool, the kind my grandmother used to give me to scrub the burnt pots. I pulled her blouse off her shoulders and it cascaded onto her desk. She pulled me toward her, her breasts rubbing against my white

Guess T-shirt. Her hand traveled down my chest toward my dick and she started to rub it through my pants.

"I had a feeling you were packing. Looks and a big dick. What more can a girl ask for?"

I helped her pull my T-shirt over my head. She started to make her way down my chest, leaving a trail of red lip marks. She unbuckled my pants and slid them down. She gently brushed the outsides of my legs with her fingertips as she reached up to pull off my Calvin Klein boxers. I stepped to the side as she gathered my clothes and put them on the couch. I stood naked on the 25th floor of an office building in the heart of Manhattan.

"You have what I want in a husband," she said as I started to remove her clothes.

I started playing with her breasts and slowly made my way down to her skirt. I lifted it up and worked my way between her legs. My right hand moved over the front of her panties. They were moist. I moved them to the side and slipped my finger inside of her. I guess my friend Brian had been right. Girlfriend was "dripping wet." I played with her for a few seconds more before I moved my hand to her butt. No disappointments there! It was perfectly rounded as advertised. She was wearing a thong. An old song played in my head, but it quickly faded, like the career of the artist who had performed it.

We continued to kiss until I flipped her around. In doing so, her hands pushed aside the things she had on her desk. I took her hand away from my dick and slid on one of the condoms that I had bought from Duane Reade earlier. I grabbed her by the hair, her weave feeling like that same steel wool, but it shredded much more. I pushed her head down in front of the desk. Her two hands held onto the desk for support. I entered her with the force and the vengeance of a man lost to both himself and the world. She screamed and rocked the desk as she spread her legs even wider for more support; pushing her butt back to meet my thrusts. As she did that, a picture fell off the desk and shattered. She was in the picture with a man and two young boys. I glanced at it and then at her butt. I slammed into her a few more times until I sent a million of my kids to their death against the walls of the rubber. She fell to the floor as I gave one last push.

"I needed that. You have a cell phone?" she asked, putting her clothes on.

Donna realized how the game was to be played. I admired that. This was not reality TV; it was the script of life.

"It's 917-777-7777."

"All those sevens?"

"It's better than three sixes."

I followed her cue and started to get dressed. She quickly put my phone number in her Palm organizer. She didn't offer hers nor did I ask for it. If any communication was going to take place, it would have to come from her. I finished dressing and headed to the door, having accomplished the job that I had set out to do. It was time for my quick exit. Hopefully both parties were satisfied but, if not, *that's life*. This wasn't going to be a long, drawn-out affair and I understood that. I didn't care to hear about her lousy life and she didn't care to hear about mine. I didn't even care if she had a happy life with her husband and kids. Even though I had just had an orgasm, my dick instantly missed the warmth of her pussy. I definitely couldn't go straight home to my wife.

"Wait for me," she said. "I have to clean up this mess and make one phone call." She started straightening the desk. "I think this is yours." She wrapped the used condom in tissues and handed it to me.

"I nearly forgot that." I placed it in my pocket. "A slip-up on my part."

Donna grinned mischievously. "If you were an NBA player, I might have kept it."

"In that case, it could either make you rich or dead."

"Yeah, I forgot it's not the sixties." She picked up the phone and dialed a number quickly. She spoke briefly in a language I didn't understand. "My husband is from South Africa."

"Speaking in tongues," I said, and sat down on the couch. It was 6:30.

She glanced down at the floor and bent down. "Damn! This is the third time this week this has happened." She threw the bits of broken glass from the picture frame into the small garbage pail and placed it back under her desk. "These ninety-nine cent stores are getting rich off me replacing frames."

I waited for her to finish and we took the elevator down to the first floor. I didn't know why she had wanted me to wait for her nor did I care.

"Good night, Mrs. August," a potbellied security guard with a heavy Grenadian accent said as we exited the building. When we got outside, there was a tall, attractive, blonde waiting for us. From the look they gave each other, I surmised that Donna wasn't finished for the evening.

"Thank you," Donna said and waved to me as she went to join the white lady, who eyed me up and down before she and Donna slipped into a black limousine waiting at the curb.

I walked two blocks south, then one east, which took me to the entrance of the Carton Bar. I went inside and, as usual, there was a combination of suits and casuals. I sat at the bar and the bartender came over.

"Hennessy on the rocks," I said.

I swiveled the chair around so that I could gaze at the rest of the people who, like me, found themselves needing a drink at seven in the evening. To my left was a white man about fifty-five years old in a postal uniform, sipping on a drink that was as clear as water. I didn't think it was water because that would mean he had to drink a lot of those little glasses before he satisfied his thirst. As if on cue, he tapped his glass and the bartender gave him a refill of what turned out to be vodka on the way to bringing my drink. A little bit farther down from him were two white boys who barely looked to be of legal drinking age. They had a pitcher of beer and about six shot glasses in front of them. They seemed to be having a good time. I looked over at the tables away from the bar and noticed a couple lost in each other's eyes or possibly simply lost in New York. Farther left from them were two young black women? my guess, neither was a day over twenty-five. They both had identical hairstyles, long golden weaves that the singer Beyonce had made so popular lately. They kept looking at me and giggling. I wondered if they were working girls. Maybe I would break a promise to myself and pay for the warmth. I could have easily made a phone call, but tonight I was in the mood for something new. I watched as one of them held what I thought was a mozzarella cheese stick, which she twirled around like a baton. I turned back and took a long sip of my drink.

I had recently turned thirty-five and had been married for four years. I had a four-year-old son and I was one of the few Blacks living in the exclusive

Mill Basin section of Brooklyn. Neither the money nor the home, valued at well over three million, kept me in Mill Basin. It was my son. I loved my son with every drop of blood that circulated through my system. He kept me alive.

"Excuse me?" I felt the slight tap on my shoulder. I put my drink down and once more swiveled in my chair. It was one of the girls I had noticed earlier. She was the bigger of the two. I guessed she was five-eight and weighed about one hundred forty-five pounds.

"Yes." My face showed no emotion.

"My friend wants to fuck you. It's her birthday."

I looked over at her friend who was holding the cheese stick. She had a big smile on her face. What she asked for didn't mean a thing to me. I had lost my virginity at the age of nine to an older woman, my grandmother's best friend's granddaughter. Her name was Cindy and she was twenty years old at the time. The only thing I remembered about her was that she had smelled like smoke.

"And you?" I asked.

"I wouldn't mind," she said, playing with my curly hair.

"How much?" I asked. My face remained emotionless. I wasn't the only one wanting warmth tonight.

She stopped playing with my hair and stood back.

"How much?" she repeated as if her repetition would dissipate the question. "Are you a whore? Because we don't want any whore."

"Do I look like a whore? And if I was, do you think you could afford me for your friend's birthday?" I pulled up my shirtsleeve and checked the time on my Movado.

She stared into my eyes. "How about both of us together?" she asked, signaling her friend, who was starting to get up.

"Been there, done that too many times. Unless your shit has gold fillings, this conversation is over."

"I'll be right back," she said and headed over to her friend.

I took a sip of my drink and rested a hundred-dollar bill under the glass. She returned shortly and put her hand around my back as if we were old friends.

I put my drink down. "Make sure you don't insult me."

"We're willing to do $400, but you have to buy a bottle of Courvoisier as a birthday gift to my friend." There was a stupid smile on her face. "Like the song..."

"I hate the song but I'll buy the bottle. Let's go."

I left the bartender with a hundred-dollar bill for a $6.50 drink. It was never about the money; it was about the game.

I drove into my driveway at Mills Lane at 10:00 p.m., parking my S500 next to the red convertible X-type Jaguar in the driveway. As I stepped onto the pavement, a large black pit bull came trotting toward me. I stooped and rubbed the dog on the top of his head. He rubbed against my pants leg, walked with me to the large French doors and stood back as I opened the door.

"Thanks for picking up Emerald from school. You didn't have to leave as soon as we came home." My wife, Lauren Carter, stood in the middle of the living room. Her right eye was black and swollen.

"Is Emerald asleep?" I asked.

"Like you care. He's been asleep since eight-thirty," she answered.

I took off my shoes and put them in the closet. "I'm taking him to the zoo tomorrow."

"Lauren, come here," a husky female voice beckoned from the kitchen.

I followed my wife, who bolted toward the voice.

"I thought I told you I don't want all that mayonnaise on my sandwich," the woman sitting at the kitchen table in a red nightgown said as my wife picked up the sandwich. That woman was my wife's lover. "You know I don't like hitting you, but you don't listen."

"Sorry, Annette, I'll do it over," my wife said.

I went to the refrigerator and took out a Heineken. As I passed by, Annette Hutchinson stood. She was a little bit shorter than Lauren and God had created her ugly.

She looked at me, challenging me with her eyes.

I opened the bottle and leaned against the counter, returning her challenge.

"What?! You want to do something about this?" She pointed to Lauren. "Go ahead and see if you won't be arrested for spousal abuse."

"Just as long as you keep your hands where they won't be cut off. If I ever come home and find my child with so much as a scratch on his arm, I'll take that artificial dick and shove it up your nose."

"Stop it! Both of you!" Lauren screamed, then lowered her voice as she added, "Donald, Dad said he wants to see you tomorrow."

I walked out of the kitchen and went up the stairs past the master bedroom into a room littered with an assortment of toys. I knelt next to the bed where my child lay fast asleep. I held the Heineken in my right hand as I used my left to move the curly hair away from his eyes. I kissed him in the middle of his forehead. A small tear escaped from my left eye onto his bed.

"I love you," I said and stood.

I left the room and headed down to the last room at the end of the hall. I put the bottle next to the cases of empty ones in the walk-in-closet. I sat by the window looking out at the darkness of the night. I knew what I had to do. Maybe the next day I could stand up to my father-in-law and tell him what I had been unable to for four years. Then maybe I could walk away from my prison of madness.

CHAPTER 2

"Emerald, come here," I called to my son as I walked toward the entrance to my father-in-law's study.

"Coming, Daddy," he answered, running to me on his active little legs.

When he was at my side, he nudged his head against my pants leg as I reached down and played with his hair. I had recently taken him to the barber, who had cut Emerald's shoulder-length hair so that it barely touched his ears. I knocked gradually against the dark cherry, wooden door.

"Come in," the baritone voice came forcibly through the door.

I opened the door cautiously.

"Grandpa!" Emerald shouted and ran into the arms of a man who had celebrated his seventieth birthday but remained as agile and fit as a forty-year-old man.

"Son," he said and turned the big, ancient-looking mahogany chair around so that Emerald could come into his arms. "How's my favorite son doing today?"

"Daddy and I are going to the Bronx Zoo," Emerald replied, holding his grandfather tightly around his neck.

My son's IQ was way beyond his tender age of four. By the age of two, he was already speaking in complete sentences. He currently attended a special school for gifted children.

"Did Grandma give you that gift I bought for you?" Dennis Malcolm, my father-in-law, asked. Even though Dennis was his first name, no one called him that, not even his wife. It was either Mr. Malcolm or Malcolm.

"No, I didn't see Grandma."

He ran his hands through Emerald's hair. "Well, you know where she is."

"Is she in the bedroom?" Emerald asked.

"No," my father-in-law answered.

"Is she in the kitchen?"

"No, and you have one more chance. Otherwise, you don't get the present."

My son looked up at his grandfather with those big, beautiful brown eyes of his and said, "She's in the garden."

"You've got it. Now, go see Grandma while your father and I talk. Donald, thanks for coming over today. How's work?" he asked.

"Work is fine, Mr. Malcolm. Thank you for the opportunity."

"Donald, you are part of the family now and family members help each other. Did you reconsider what we spoke about last week? As you know, I'm not young anymore and my daughter is definitely not making any more kids. I'm even willing to let you divorce my daughter. You could go on your merry way, a rich man."

"There's no reconsideration, Mr. Malcolm. I'm not changing my son's last name from Edison to Malcolm. And there isn't enough money in the world to make me leave my son."

Mr. Malcolm leaned forward in the chair, interlocking his hands.

"Donald, you know my wife doesn't like you. She has always felt that you married our daughter for the money."

"I didn't…"

"Don't interrupt, Donald; especially when I know she's right. I see the way women ogle you. You can get any woman you want. I don't believe you took one look at my daughter and said to yourself, 'This is the woman I want to spend the rest of my life with.' After you two were engaged, I had a detective follow you from that very day until the day you walked down that aisle. You never went one week without being unfaithful to my daughter, but that's not important. You're an opportunist and I can't fault that."

He cleared his throat.

That break gave me the opportunity to wipe the sweat that had begun to form on my forehead. I hated being in that position. I felt weak and defenseless.

"Can I have a drink?" I asked, hoping to end the conversation. I suddenly realized that I would never get what I had come there to ask for.

Mr. Malcolm picked up the phone and spoke briefly into it.

"I see you're not interested in talking about your love for my daughter, so we shall move on. I offered you five hundred-thousand dollars the last time you were here, to change your son's surname to mine and you refused. Today, I'm willing to offer you a million dollars and a condo on Miami's South Beach. What do you say, Donald? One million dollars transferred into the bank of your choosing; no strings attached." He smiled, his cosmetically whitened teeth glistening.

My voice trembled with anger. "Sir, I told you before and I'll tell you once more, my son is not for sale."

"Donald, why don't you think about it? I recognize the fact that you have nothing. The car you drive belongs to my corporation. The house you live in is owned by my daughter. Even the platinum American Express card belongs to the corporation. A man has to own something, Donald, or else he's not a man. When I was your age…"

Here he goes again, explaining my failures and extolling his virtues. I purposely rolled my eyes in my head. He ignored my action and continued.

"Life was never easy for me. Granted, my father was a rich man, but he made sure that I worked hard to understand the importance of earning your keep. After graduating from Howard University where I received my MBA, he started me in management. There was no preferential treatment given to me because I was his son. Sometimes I wished that I were back in college with the Benz and access to unlimited cash. He warned me that it would stop when I graduated, and it did."

I looked over at the clock; it was after four. I doubted I would be able to get to the zoo with Emerald, but I planned to try.

"From that time on, I had to work for everything I got."

There was a welcomed knock on the door.

"Come in," Malcolm said.

A maid dressed in a black and white uniform came in with a tray with two glasses, a carton of orange juice and a bottle of cranberry juice. Malcolm pointed to the cranberry juice and the maid poured him a glass. I strained to see her face because I wasn't sure that I had met her before.

"Orange juice," I said, making sure I didn't drink the same thing he was drinking. I needed something stronger, but whenever I drove with Emerald, I tried not to drink any alcohol.

She poured the juice, turned around and gave it to me. I recognized her. Her name was Jessica and I had fucked her in the garden two weeks before my wedding. She looked at me, her eyes unwavering, as she put the juice carton back on the tray and left it on the table.

"Anything else, Sir?" she asked Malcolm. He shook his head and she quickly left the room, quietly closing the door behind her.

"She gives a great blow job," Mr. Malcolm said. "I guess you don't know about that because all you did was fuck her in the garden."

I had taken a big gulp of the orange juice that had now made its way through my nose in an unflattering display of shock.

"Donald, Donald, you fail to realize the power of money." He handed me a tissue from the box on his desk.

I took it and wiped my nose, rolling the tissue in a ball and reaching over and dumping it in the small, empty wastebasket.

"You knew all this about me and you allowed me to marry your daughter?"

"Donald, my only child is a lesbian. I have tried to deny that ever since the time my wife caught her kissing her girlfriend; she had just turned fifteen. I did everything to get her away from women with those tendencies. Throughout high school I paid so many young men to take her on dates. Do you know what it's like to be a multimillionaire with one child and have that child be a lesbian? Now you see why you're such a Godsend."

There he was, so calmly admitting that he had played me for a fool. One of the main reasons I had married Lauren was because she wasn't too interested in sex. For me, that was perfect. That way, I would have the time of my life fucking everything I could find.

I stared directly into Malcolm's cold, calculating eyes. "So, you played me for a fool."

He returned my stare without blinking. His old, cagey eyes sent a chill through my body. "I did no such thing. You saw a golden opportunity to have your cake and eat it too, so you went for it. But the cake you went for happens not to be what you expected."

I took a deep breath and said, "I want out. I don't want your money or anything. I simply want to take my son and get out."

Malcolm started to laugh as if I had made the finals on BET's *Comic View*. After about a minute went by, he stopped as suddenly as he had begun. "You're not serious, are you?"

"Yes," I said, resisting the urge to jump over the table and snap his fucking neck.

"First, you're not going anywhere. Second, even if you leave, you will be leaving without my grandson. He's the only person that I'm living for right now. You and my daughter don't mean anything to me. If you're thinking of running away with him, forget it. There isn't a place on this earth you can go that I wouldn't be able to find you. So, unless you plan to take the money and exit the marriage, my advice to you is to continue to fuck those whores and go home and play pretend husband."

There was a loud noise outside the study, as if someone was driving a car in the house. The door slid open and my mother-in-law, Dora Malcolm, poked her head in.

"As you can tell, he got your present," Dora said, barely acknowledging me with a nod.

"Daddy, look what Grandpa bought for me," Emerald said, getting out of a miniature car. "Can I drive it in the house at home?"

I half-heartedly looked at the toy, rage boiling under my skin. "No, Emerald, but you can drive it in the driveway and the back yard," I said, reaching down to turn the engine off.

"Okay." He took the key from my hand and placed it in his jeans pocket. "This is my key," he said proudly.

"Dora, Malcolm, we'll be leaving now," I said, unable to look at Malcolm.

"Emerald, come give Grandpa a kiss before you go," Malcolm said and bent down as Emerald ran to him.

"I love you, Grandpa," he said.

"And me?" Dora asked.

Emerald went from his grandfather's chest to his grandmother's arms. "You too, Grandma," he said with an equal amount of conviction.

"I'll have Ray drop the car off later," Malcolm said.

"Why can't we take it, Daddy?"

"It's too big to fit in our car," I answered, taking him by the hand and starting to walk down the hall.

"Don't worry, Emerald, the car will be home before you get there," Dora said.

Dora was right. I had no intentions of going straight home. I pulled my car out from between the Bentley and the white Porsche convertible in the driveway. I made a few turns before ending up on Avenue U. My son eagerly talked about his new car as I headed onto the Belt Parkway. I had buckled him up in the back seat with his Game Boy. At half past four, the Belt Parkway was beginning to get a bit crowded. The grand opening of the new mall between Kings Plaza and JFK wasn't helping either. The Benz responded quickly as I touched my foot to the gas pedal. My days of doing a buck twenty-five on the Belt were over. These days I was carrying a precious cargo.

"Daddy, are we going to Aunty Julie's before we go to the zoo?" Emerald asked, staring out the window.

"Yes, Emerald, we're going to Aunt Julie's."

"Is she going to the zoo with us?

"I don't know, but I'm going to ask her to come with us," I replied as I took the exit ramp at exit 22. After multiple twists and turns, I pulled up behind a blue Toyota Camry on a block filled with single-family homes. As is true of most Queens neighborhoods, the block was very quiet with the exception of a few people walking their dogs or pre-teens riding on the sidewalk. I unbuckled my son's seat belt and hoisted him up onto my shoulders.

"Hello, Emerald," Julie said, coming to greet us at the door.

Julie had recently celebrated her thirtieth birthday. She was five feet seven inches tall with an olive complexion. The smile that she gave to my son lifted me into the clouds. Julie had always been there for me. I had met her during my sophomore year in college and she was the only woman from college that I had kept in contact with on a regular basis. She was a wizard in mathematics, tutoring me through my battle with Calculus. As junior partner of one of the largest accounting firms on Wall Street, she commanded a salary of $195,000. She had purchased her house about five years earlier, making the migration from a small $1,500 studio apartment in Clinton Hill in Brooklyn.

"Are you hungry?" she asked me, taking Emerald into her arms and carrying him into the house.

"Daddy said we're going to the zoo," Emerald said as I pulled the door shut.

"Well, if your dad said we're going to the zoo, then we're going to the zoo," Julie replied as she put Emerald down. "Do you want something to eat first?"

I had already gone to the refrigerator and taken out a bottle of Poland Spring water.

"I don't," Emerald said. "I ate at Grandma's."

"I sure didn't eat at Grandma's. I'm famished."

"What does famished mean, Daddy?"

"It's another way of saying that I'm very hungry, Emerald."

"Where's Linky?" Emerald asked. Linky was Julie's cat. Emerald loved him. I wasn't in a hurry to see him.

"I think he went outside," Julie said. "I'm sure he'll be back later."

"Emerald, I'm going to eat in the kitchen," I said.

"Okay, Daddy," Emerald replied, sitting in front of the television. "Aunty Julie, can I watch the cartoon channel?"

I lifted the cover off a pot on the stove, steam escaped. I took two spoons of rice, then headed for the stewed chicken. The smell alone made me want to eat the entire bowl. I packed chicken legs and breasts onto my plate. There was potato salad with chopped, boiled eggs and green peppers. I used the knife to cut two cubes of the macaroni pie. Finally, I leaned back onto one of the black seats surrounding the table and started on the overfilled plate.

"I see that you *are* very hungry," Julie said, as she walked into the kitchen. "Father and son, what a pair! One is busy stuffing his face and the other is fast asleep." She paused. "Donald, when are you going to stop this?"

I put the fork down and looked up at Julie. There was concern etched between those beautiful high brows. I knew exactly what she was talking about. I hadn't eaten dinner in my own house for more than two years.

"He's all that I live for. If it was only about walking away from the wealth, I would've done that a long time ago. There's no way that I'm going to leave my son to grow up with those two bitches."

"Donald, it's all your fault. You said you wanted a meal ticket. You said you didn't want to marry for love and all that other stuff."

"I got what I wanted, but things have changed. There is so much more. Sometimes I laugh at myself, the man who could get almost any woman he wants ends up with a woman who doesn't want him. How ironic!" I dug my fork into the potato salad.

"So what? Now you're going to give up and waste your life drowning yourself in the stupor of alcohol."

I smiled. Julie was the only person I knew who used the English language in such a formal way.

"Today, I told him I wanted out." I reluctantly placed the fork down. "And you know what he told me?"

"What?"

"He told me I could leave but I had to leave my son. He told me what I realized all along; he doesn't care about his daughter or me. But, before that, he raised the price on my son's head. He offered me a million dollars to change my son's last name. Do you believe that?" I asked, gazing into Julie's eyes.

"Donald, did you think he would stop asking to change your son's last name? Your father-in-law has it all, except an heir to his fortune. He's a businessman who's willing to pay whatever the cost to get what he wants. Right now, he wants his grandson. I've only met that man once and he gave me the creeps." Julie ran her hands up and down her elbows.

"Julie, I have to get out. I don't know how I'm going to do it, but I can't raise my son in this situation. He's young now, but he'll sense the hate soon and I don't want to guess what that's going to do to him. I can't live in that house anymore."

Julie came over and placed her hand over my head. She took my head and leaned it against her side. I wrapped my arm around her waist. For the first time that day, I felt at peace. I was secure in the arms of my best friend.

CHAPTER 3

The Brooklyn Marriott was located on Adam Street, a block away from the Brooklyn Bridge. I drove down Atlantic Avenue and turned onto Adam. Taking the local road, I made a right into the underground parking garage. The attendant stopped my car and came over to make his inspection. He asked me to open the trunk and he quickly looked inside. He glanced in the back seat as if expecting to see a big timer with a "BOMB" label. I took the ticket from him and parked my car.

The escalator ascended to the second floor where I made a left into the main dining room. The hostess, a young woman in her early twenties, looked at me as if she was about to have her favorite dessert. She pushed her chest out a little further than necessary, making sure I saw her hard nipples tight against her white shirt.

"Good evening, Sir. Will you be dining by yourself this evening?" she asked as if making a wish.

"Donald, I see you made it on time."

I turned around to see Donna in tight, dirty jeans, which from the front promised a lot behind. She had no need to push out her chest because her breasts made their own voluptuous statement.

She slipped her hand around my waist, reached up and gave me a kiss on the cheek.

I turned back around to the hostess. Her chest had become flat and the smile she had greeted me with earlier had disappeared.

"Table for two?" she asked.

I nodded in agreement.

"Follow me." She picked up two menus and walked away.

I followed her, knowing that pairs of eyes would be dissecting us as we walked to the table.

"Will this table be good for you?" the hostess asked. Her name tag said Lisa.

"Thank you, Lisa; this will be fine," I replied.

The earlier smile that had disappeared when Donna walked in came back with a vengeance. "Your waiter will be over shortly. Feel free to come over and ask me anything you want to know about our hotel. We're presently offering a twenty percent discount on rooms for corporate accounts." She walked away, putting as much swing as possible into her pancake butt.

"Why didn't she just give you the keys to the room?" Donna stated with sarcasm.

"A little jealous?" I joked.

"Jealous, not really," she said, taking the menu and opening it up.

"Good afternoon, Sir, Madam." The waiter was a middle-aged white man with a deep, Russian accent. "Can I get you something to drink while you peruse the menu?"

"No, thank you. We'll order in a minute," I said.

"Where do they get these people from? We haven't sat down a minute and they're in your face. Didn't he see us looking at the menus?" Donna said, sounding exasperated.

"We're obviously not at the Waldorf in Manhattan," I answered, noticing the waiter standing a few feet away staring at me.

"Should we drink the water and leave?" Donna asked, returning the waiter's penetrating gaze. "Or should I order the chicken sandwich? It looks delicious."

"I've had it before. It's very good. Today I think I'll have the salmon sandwich. It's difficult to mess up salmon." I closed the menu.

"You obviously haven't been to Fish and Things on Jessup Avenue. I had the worst salmon in my life there," she replied, putting down her menu.

I lifted my right hand up and the waiter hurried over. I placed the order for both of us, repeating it twice as the waiter fumbled with his pen.

"What's the occasion? This isn't our usual meeting place," I said, as our eyes connected.

I had fucked Donna four more times since our initial encounter in the office. Unlike the first encounter, those sessions were long and exciting. I had put in some wonderful work on that woman.

"It's time," she said.

The waiter had remembered and placed the correct dishes in front of us.

"Will that be all? Something to drink?" he asked.

"Water is fine," Donna answered.

"We have bottled water, if you would like."

"Just leave us alone," I finally said, beginning to get annoyed.

"Call me if you need anything," he replied and disappeared behind the large door leading to the kitchen.

"He's pissing me off!" Donna said, separating her precut sandwich into two halves.

"Time for what?" I brought her back to her original statement.

"Donald, did you think that I got together with you because of your looks?" she asked. "Yeah, I'm sure you did. You put me in the cage with those chicken-heads out there."

"I didn't put you anywhere," I said; not liking where our conversation was headed.

"Of course you didn't, but all you men do the same thing."

I was curious. "What's that?"

"Think with your dicks and lie with your mouth. Donald, let me give you some advice. Never fool yourself into thinking that you know what a woman wants." She bit into her sandwich.

I wasn't expecting anything but occasional sex from Donna. She never once mentioned anything else. She would call me and, if I was available, I would go. We rarely talked about our home lives and we had completed the project at her office.

She showed her hearty appetite by tearing into the sandwich. I looked at her as she ate, making sure that she chewed completely before swallowing. And when she did swallow, everything was gone. I began getting excited by mentally replacing my dick for the food.

"Your dick is thinking again," she said. "How's your wife?"

"The same as your husband, I suppose."

"He's at home, happy in bed, waiting for me to come to the house and fuck him until he pledges undying love to me," she said, a soft smile forming on her perfectly shaped lips. "Is your wife at home picking pussy hairs from between her teeth?"

"What do you know about my wife?"

"I know she likes the beaver more than she likes the dog."

"And?"

"How did you happen to have Emerald? By the way, he looks exactly like you. Was she drunk that night?" Donna said, finishing up the fries that came with the sandwich.

"What do you want from me?" I asked, feeling like the only one naked in this conversation.

"The only time you used your head for the right thing, you ended up getting fucked, didn't you?" Donna started on the other half of the sandwich.

I finished the first half of mine and pushed it away from the table.

"Only a man would get caught up with a lesbian. You should have known by the way she looked at your dick that she preferred pussy. I realized that from the first time I met her. Why did you think she kept her eyes focused on you? Do you think it was because she was so much in love? No, my friend, it was the only way for her not to stare at women."

"When did you meet my wife?"

"Is that important?" she asked.

"Maybe."

"It's terrible living at home, isn't it? On one hand, there's your son whose blood runs in you. On the other, your wife and her abusive lover whom you despise. Poor Donald; he doesn't even own the car he drives. Is that enough?" she asked.

"If there's more, feel free to continue," I said, looking at her empty plate. It seemed like the entire world had me undressed.

"It's time," Donna said, eyeing my half-eaten sandwich.

I pushed my plate toward her. "On second thought, take this bullshit home to your husband."

Donna's face became contorted. "You ready to go upstairs?"

"What's upstairs for me?"

"Freedom for you and your son; if you play your cards right."

"The cost?"

"Maybe nothing; maybe everything. It's your choice. You can get up and walk out right now and continue to live life as usual. Or you can go up to the room with me and take a chance at freedom. I'll be in suite 531." She drank the rest of the water and motioned for the waiter to come over. She signed for the check and walked out of the restaurant.

The elevator took me to the fifth floor. Donna and I had never been to this hotel but, in the relatively short time it had been open, I had been here on five occasions; each time with a different woman. The last time had been with Nicole, a doctor at Kings County Hospital in Brooklyn. Nicole had recently moved to Clinton Hill and, after numerous dates with men labeled "assholes" by her, we had connected at the newly opened Susan's Cafe on Flatbush Avenue.

My shoes sank down into the plush red carpet as I exited the elevator. Arrows pointed both right and left with various ranges of room numbers. Suite 531 was the last room on the right; next to an exit door. As I walked down the hallway, I wondered exactly what Donna had in mind for me. I knocked three times on the door and waited. I had never been nervous about entering a hotel room, but there was something different that day. It seemed that I would be expected to do more than stick my dick in a piece of pussy.

"The door is open. Come in and lock it behind you," I heard Donna say through the thick door.

I turned the knob and walked in. The light in the hallway reflected against a mirrored closet. I stopped and glanced at myself in the mirror. My stomach felt a little pudgy from the meal, but it was not reflected in the mirror. I ran my fingers through my hair before proceeding. The living room had a desk and two sofas. There was an additional table with four chairs; for meetings,

I assumed. I heard two women's voices coming from behind a closed door located on the left side of the room.

Donna's voice, the softer of the two, came from behind the doors. "We're in here."

I pulled the door open and stepped into the bedroom. Donna was seated on the bed in a short nightgown that didn't cover much. Her back was against the headboard and in her hand was a full glass of what I presumed to be liquor. Her long legs extended off the bed into the lap of the same white woman that I had seen the first time Donna and I had fucked at her job. The white woman's glass was half-empty. I looked over at the bottle chilling in the bucket. It was a bottle of Dom Perignon and next to it was a glass filled with ice.

Donna extended her hand toward the white woman. "Donald, this is Kathleen."

"Donald, Donna has told me so much about you," Kathleen said, pushing out her right hand to mine.

"Is that so?" I said, taking her hand and kissing it. "Anything worth proving?"

"Not necessarily worth proving, but definitely worth experiencing," she said, putting down her glass and taking the one next to the bucket and filling it up.

"Come, Donald, sit on the bed." Donna gestured to the space vacated by Kathleen. I sat down on the firm, king-sized bed as Kathleen handed me a drink.

"You like Dom Perignon?" she asked as she went over to the dresser and leaned on it.

"Anything but Cristal. It seems once a rapper puts a drink in a song the drink becomes diluted," I replied.

"Donna wasn't sure that you'd come, but I think she teased you enough. They say if you tease a man, he will go to the ends of the earth to find out what's behind it. In this case, all you had to do was take the elevator to the fifth floor." Kathleen twirled her drink with her finger, then sucked the liquid from it.

"Are we fucking, planning an assassination, or are we going to sit here and bullshit?" I asked, looking over at Kathleen's creamy thighs and her pencil-thin lips that I could imagine impaled on Donna's labia.

"What's the rush, Donald? You're not invited to the party at home," Donna said, running her fingers over her nipples. "We're here for a lot more than fucking. Pussies and dicks are a dime a dozen; as you know. This here is a lifetime opportunity. I picked you because I know your history and, as the junk emails would say, you need a change."

Donna took her toes and ran them down the back of my head.

"I'm listening," I said as Kathleen, with those long, beautiful legs and blonde pussy hairs, approached the bed. I had heard that a lot of white woman dyed their pubic hair.

"It's not dyed," she said, as if reading my mind.

"I'm not selling shampoo, so I really don't care," I replied as I pulled her toward me.

Donna reached over my shoulders and started to loosen my shirt.

"What would you do for freedom?" Donna said, as she ran her hands down my T-shirt.

"There are many jails. I don't want to exchange mine for another one."

"I think you were right, Donna. He is the right one," Kathleen said as she shoved her right nipple into my mouth. I sucked on it slowly, occasionally biting it to make her wince. I reached my hand around, grabbed a handful of Kathleen's hair and pulled her down to her knees.

She unbuckled my pants and swiftly yanked both them and my boxers off. By now my penis had already risen to the occasion.

"We're planning a robbery," Donna whispered in my ear.

Kathleen was all gums.

"How much?" I asked, standing, and in the process taking my dick out of Kathleen's mouth.

"Twenty million dollars in untraceable bonds," Kathleen said, her mouth finally free to speak.

I took my right hand and grabbed her shiny, bouncing blonde hair, and as I lifted her up, I took my left hand and pushed Donna back down on the bed. I don't know if I pushed Kathleen between Donna's legs or if Donna's pussy lips were a vacuum. All I know was that air couldn't separate Kathleen's mouth from Donna's pussy.

"Who is it?" I asked, running my hands over Kathleen's white ass. I slid my fingers between the furls of her blonde pubic hair. The liquid from her wetness trailed down my finger like a wet sponge. I wiped my hands on the bed and pulled out the green Trojan condoms that had become my trademark. I slipped my fingers back into Kathleen and used her juices to add extra lubrication to the condom. Pussy eating wasn't my thing. If a woman wanted her pussy eaten, she could find another woman to do that. I was here for one thing only and that was my dick. I tapped Kathleen on her *Lucille Roberts* twice-a-week exercised ass and she spread her legs to allow maximum penetration.

"We want you to rob my boss, Kathleen's husband," Donna said as I sent my dick into Kathleen's depths. I should have stopped fucking, put on my clothes and gotten the fuck out of there. That was the wise thing to do.

I didn't do the wise thing. "Is he carrying?"

I continued to go in and out of Kathleen, alternating between short strokes and long to the point of coming out and back inside of her. Her moans were muffled by her mouth being deep into Donna.

"He's scared of guns, but he's well-connected—they will be close. Timing is everything. Something goes wrong and we are dead."

The only person who was out of this conversation was Kathleen and it was obvious why.

"What's the split? Not saying that I'm interested, but I need to know the split."

Donna was pushing her butt up in the air as Kathleen continued to do her thing.

"Sixty-forty. Kathleen doesn't care. She's got money and nothing can come her way."

"So what's in it for her?" I asked, as if Kathleen wasn't even there.

"Seeing that fucker suffer." Kathleen took her mouth away from Donna's twat for a few seconds. "I want to stab him in the back. If he gets crippled, he's not going anywhere.

My dick evaporated faster than the chemical weapons in Iraq.

"Peter wants to divorce me. Who does he think he is?" Kathleen said with an angry scowl on her face. The long bouncing blonde hair had become matted from our activities. "He wants to give me up over some bitch he claims to be in love with. I've done everything that man asked me to do. I did the wife-swapping thing. He introduced me to eating pussy; and this is my reward. I don't care who he fucks, but don't end the relationship over some bitch."

"After we're finished with him, he won't leave you," Donna chimed in.

"Do you know what it's like to be divorced in the suburbs? If you're not Mrs. Whatever, you're nothing. It's like having AIDS in the eighties. I can't let him leave me," she said, burying her head on the table and sobbing uncontrollably.

Donna hugged Kathleen as the woman wept and that led to Donna sliding down on the chair in front of Kathleen. My dick got hard again and I slipped on another condom. I slid down between Donna's feet so as not to interrupt them. I lifted her ass up and she dropped down onto my dick. A floor below us, they were lifting weights, while I was up here lifting ass.

Kathleen made her exit about half an hour after our "second coming." I watched as Donna started to get her stuff together.

"I have to meet my husband at Carnegie Hall. Our daughter's performing," she stated casually.

I picked up the two spent condoms and stuffed them into a small plastic bag.

"So how long have you been fucking Kathleen's husband, Peter?" I asked.

"Not just a pretty face after all," Donna said as she slipped on a blue skirt.

"If you thought that, you wouldn't have invited me up to the room," I said, flushing the condoms down the toilet bowl. I don't know why I put them into the plastic wrap before I flushed them, but I did.

"White men and black pussy, they just don't know how to act. I'm not leaving my husband for any soft-ass white man. The gifts are good, but that's it. I love my husband. He's a good man and an exemplary father. I give this man a taste and he's getting stupid. He told me a few months ago that he was thinking about leaving Kathleen. I told him that it wasn't a good idea because it would mess everything up. But no, he goes and tells Kathleen he wants a divorce anyway." Donna completed her outfit with a white blouse. She took the clothes that she was wearing earlier and dumped them in the garbage can.

I looked at her and the garbage. She smiled.

I smiled. Sometimes garbage is garbage.

She answered my inquisitive look. "That's why men always get caught. They don't do the math. My husband or a hundred dollars' worth of clothes."

"What if…"

"I've been with my husband for over ten years. Do you honestly believe that he's paying attention to what I put on in the morning? But let me come home smelling like I just got fucked."

I looked at the rest of the liquor in the bottle. "Do what you have to do."

"You might as well stay the night," Donna said as she picked up her bag. "The suite is paid for."

I went back to the bed and took the sheets off. I picked up the phone and dialed room service.

"You're not done, are you?" Donna asked as she opened the suite door.

"Not by a long shot. I'm going downstairs to get some dinner," I said as my stomach started to growl.

"Just keep our discussion to yourself."

"Go meet your husband," I said, irritated because she seemed like she was calling me a bitch.

"Maybe I'll have him eat me out in the bathroom at Carnegie Hall. You know you men are always wanting to push the envelope," she said as she closed the door.

CHAPTER 4

I picked up the Heineken bottle and dumped it in the small round white garbage can Brian had in the kitchen.

"Donald, don't you ever get any feelings for women?"

I froze with my hand extended to the door.

"I think I need another beer for this." I turned back toward the kitchen table. He had asked me a question that I had all the right answers to. Brian put another Heineken in front of me.

Brian poured himself some apple juice and sat down opposite me. "I know you've been with lawyers, doctors and multimillionaires. One had to have tugged on your heart strings."

"Brian, do you know the difference between a fat woman and a skinny woman in bed?"

Brian smiled. "I would sleep with one and not the other."

"No, Brian, there isn't a fucking difference. Once you get past the size and looks, your dick feels the same way in either one of them. Have you ever noticed that some of the girls you expect to have a great time in bed with are lousy fucks?" I drank some of the Heiny...

"But sometimes that's a personality thing," he said defensively.

"Yeah, you're right, but you wait to find out." I looked through the small kitchen window into nothingness. "With me, Brian, I already know what the pussy's gonna feel like before I get in there. There ain't a damn thing a woman can do that will make that feeling change."

"Someone fucked you over really well."

It was my turn to smile. The whole world was filled with therapeutic couches and the end result was still the same. The world was fucked up.

"No, Brian, I don't think my heart has ever been broken. I've never cried over a woman or spent sleepless nights thinking about a woman. My son, yes, I have."

"Man, in this life, love is all we got. Without it, we are animals," Brian said.

"Let me tell you what my grandmother told me before I turned fifteen. She thought I hadn't started getting my dick warm yet, but I had. I listened anyway."

"So you've lived your entire life based on what your grandmother told you?" he asked.

"Her advice has stood the test of time and experience."

"I definitely want to hear this."

"She told me that in this world there are whores, pimps and johns."

"Your grandmother told you that when you were fifteen?"

"Yeah, she did."

"What did she mean?"

"Brian, think of all your relationships and you'll see that in all of them you have been either a whore, a pimp or a john."

Brian looked around the room for answers. "Go ahead. Keep talking."

"You see what separates the pimp from the john is feelings and, at any point, the pimp could be the john. In the game, a man who's in control is always the pimp. The john, therefore, is trying to be the pimp but first he has to go through the whore. All men want to be the pimp, but the whore is the most important part of this equation because she can break down either the pimp or the john. She's already broken the john because he has to come to her. You feel me?"

Brian looked at me. "You are motherfucking crazy."

Brian wasn't listening as much as he was fighting and that was sad. He wanted to be in another game other than the one he was living in. He was holding on to hope. The short rope of love; in other words, a blind man's precipice.

"The pimp has no feelings for his whore. The day he develops feelings for her is the day he loses everything, including her, and then he becomes a john. And that's what she wants."

"And the john?"

"The john wants the whore but the whore can't be his until he becomes the pimp. The john, in essence, is subservient to the whore. He has to take what she gives. The pimp, on the other hand, takes from the whore. The whore means absolutely nothing to him."

"May God have mercy on you if you ever have a female child."

I looked down at the table. "I can't change the world if I have a female child. All I can do is convey knowledge to her and my job is done."

"So you're a pimp?" he asked as I once more got up from the table.

My eyes became cloudy as if the sun had made way for Katrina. "In life, sometimes you are all three, and right now, I'm at that point in my life. I'm a pimp because I listened to my grandmother. I'm a whore because I get fucked every time I go home and I'm a john because I'm trying to go through a whore to become a pimp." I reached for the door.

"You all right?" Brian asked.

"No, but one day I will be."

I took a seat at the back of the restaurant, away from the incoming traffic. I was seated in the shadows of life and time, light casting recognition on one part of me, the other part needing closer observation. The waitress, a shapely young black woman in her early twenties, wearing tight-fitting black pants and a tee with the restaurant logo on it, presented her attributes to me.

"Hello, Sir, my name is Leila. Can I get you something?" she asked, whipping her writing pad from her back pocket.

"What are you offering?" I took her eyes in mine.

She presented the menu to me. "This."

I didn't look at it. "What else?"

"Something that's off the menu?" she asked, smiling.

"It depends on whether there's a cost associated with it." I reached out to pick up the menu.

"Everything in life has a cost. It depends on when you're planning to pay."

I liked her. "Leila, let me have a Heineken."

"That's all?"

"Yeah, for now. Maybe I'll add to that later on." I noticed a white man who had just walked into the bar.

"Do you want to make a preemptive strike?" she asked seductively.

"Maybe later on but, for now, add on a Budweiser and some privacy."

She gave me the 'who do you think you are' look and walked away, showing me what black men's dreams are made of.

I got up and shook Bill's hand. Bill was a skinny white retired NYC detective that I had hired. He had recently called me and informed me that he had located my father. The swab he had taken was a 99.9 percent match with the DNA of this old white man. He gave me a brown envelope containing pictures of my father and all of the pertinent information about him.

"Your old man is a work of art," Bill said, taking a seat opposite me.

"How so?"

"Let's just say age has done nothing to calm him down." Bill leaned away from the table as the waitress put the drinks down.

She gave me an eye lashing, or an invitation, and quickly removed herself from our presence. I reached into my jacket pocket, took out a small brown envelope and handed it to Bill. It was the balance of the twenty thousand dollars I had promised him to complete the job.

I opened the envelope and pulled out the pictures of my father. My father was a tall, old man whose face seemed to have been battered by life. His eyes were red and droopy as if alcohol had been his best companion for many years. I pushed the pictures back into the envelope for fear that the anger building up inside of me would become visible.

"Did you bring the other thing?" I asked, hoping that there was no detectable cracking in my voice.

"Donald, we've become almost friends through our transaction. While I can't empathize with you, I do understand the hurt. Now, remember, you have a child and that means you have a responsibility to that child. It's not my place to tell you what to do. My job is done here but I don't want to see you get hurt. Whatever you do, do it carefully. I've put some additional information in the package for a one-on-one meeting with your father.

Whatever you do, make sure you cover your tracks. There's a lot of hate in your father and you'll certainly encounter that when you meet him. Be careful."

I felt a slight touch on my knee and Bill motioned for me to reach under the table. I reached down and I felt the cold steel of the 9 millimeter handgun in my hand. In my other hand, he placed a box of shells. Excitement ran through my veins, as I became empowered by the life-ending piece of machinery in my possession.

"This is powerful." I slipped it into my waistband and quickly buttoned my jacket.

"I've preloaded it for you so you have to be very careful. Here are instructions and everything else you need to know to shoot and maintain this gun. The safety is on so there's no danger of an accidental firing. Remember, guns don't kill people; people shoot guns that kill people." Bill stopped to take a swig of his beer.

I flipped through the manual. "This reads like an owner's manual for a new DVD player or something."

"I don't think they make DVDs that kill people as yet. But all the information you have in your hand is available on the internet."

"Here you go." I gave Bill another envelope containing $2,000 for the gun. He put it in his pocket.

"Are you going to count it?" I asked.

"When doing certain transactions, you never count. I don't think you'll short me a buck or two."

"I wouldn't."

"Well, it was a pleasure doing business with you and feel free to contact me if you need some more assistance." Bill stretched his hand out.

I shook Bill's hand and watched as he went from shade to light. In his wake he had not only left me with answers to my troubled life but also with questions of what to do with the answers. I had already paid for the drinks so I left a ten-dollar bill on the table for the tip. As I was walking out the door, I looked over at the waitress who was conversing with the bartender. Her looks and the revealing clothes she wore got her attention; for how long depended on the giver of the attention. Maybe, for some, the attention was only for the night. For others, it might be the possible replacement for a lifeless love at home. And there was always that one person who would want to take her into his world. To me, she would only be good if she got me through the night. Yeah, all I wanted was to get through the night and wake up to see another day. I smiled at her and she waved at me. Yeah, she understood; time had decided.

It was nine-thirty when I walked into my house, eager to hide the gun.

"You're home early."

"You motherfucker," I said as I leapt over to Annette, pulling the gun out of my waistband and hitting her on the forehead. She fell to the floor, butt-naked, shattering the wine glass she had in her hand. The long black strap-on dildo lay pointing up in the air as a small flow of blood trickled from her head.

"You bitch," I said as I saw Lauren run and kneel down by Annette's side. "I told you I don't want this shit around my child. You've already confused the boy enough."

"Emerald's asleep," Lauren whimpered, trying to revive Annette.

"Daddy!" my son cried out.

"Emerald, get dressed. Your daddy is coming up."

Slowly, Annette started to come around.

"You could've killed her," Lauren said.

"Next time, I might." I headed up the stairs. "I'm taking Emerald."

Lauren lifted Annette up. "No, you can't."

"Try to stop me."

Lauren glared at me and returned to taking care of Annette.

I could have committed at least two murders and had not a single regret.

My son was still groggy when we came back down the stairs. Lauren had covered Annette with a black robe.

I walked toward the front door. "We'll be back for our things."

"Daddy, but Mommy…" Emerald ran to Lauren. They hugged and she kissed him.

"Go with your daddy. I'll see you later."

Lauren watched me with hate-filled eyes. I returned the same look.

"Go to the car, Emerald. I'll be right there."

"Daddy, where are we going?" Emerald asked, moving to the door.

"Go to the car," I repeated.

When the door was shut, I turned to Lauren; my face strained with anger.

"You should've killed me," Annette said, holding a green towel around her head.

"Next time, I promise that I will." I was glad to make that promise. "I'll be back for our clothes.

"You'll be back all right. You'll be back with my son and living right in that room down the hall," Lauren said, picking up the phone.

The gun in my waist nudged at my skin. Two bullets were all it would take. I would walk up to both of them and calmly put a bullet in each of their foreheads, turn around and walk out the house. I would get into the car and drive until my tank was empty.

I shook my head and walked out of the house. In my life, timing was everything, and tonight was not that time. There would come a time when things would change, but I had to make sure I followed the blueprint.

"Is he asleep?" I asked Julie as she walked back into the living room.

"Yes." She looked at me in dismay. "I don't know how much that little boy can take."

"It wasn't my fault." I threw my hands up in the air. "How can that bitch walk around the house at 9:30 P.M., naked except for a strap-on dildo? What happens if my son comes to the refrigerator for a drink or something? This shit will only happen over my dead body. As long as I'm alive, I won't let this happen to my son."

"But, Donald, you have zero control over what happens when you're not there. And, most of the time, you're not home. You're always out there in bed with some woman."

"I'm not at home because that would mean looking at those bitches for a lot longer than I care to. Don't you think I want to be home with my son?" I was starting to get angry with Julie.

"Don't give me that look." Julie pointed at me as she took a seat. "I didn't put you in this situation."

"I know you didn't." I motioned for her to sit by me.

She remained motionless in the chair across the room. "I don't think that's a good idea."

"Why?"

"I don't know, but Brian and I are really working out. I don't think that I could be the kind of friend I used to be with you."

"Fuck, how long have we been friends?" I asked, rising from the couch, blood circulating in my body at an orgasmic level.

"Don't act like that, Donald. It's not necessary."

"If it's not necessary, then tell me what is necessary. You're starting to get dick from this brother now and, all of a sudden, I'm nobody to you."

"Donald, I know you've had a rough evening so I'll keep Emerald here. I think you should go," she said, walking to the door.

"Go where?"

"Donald, with the amount of female friends you have, I seriously doubt that you'll be homeless tonight." She left the door open and came back to sit on the chair.

I rose and took the keys that I had laid on the foyer table when I had walked in. The door shook for a few seconds after I slammed it. I got into the Benz and headed onto the Belt Parkway. My life was a mess and wrapping around a tree at a speed of over 120 mph would have only emitted a small sound of displeasure from me. But they say if it's not your time you ain't going nowhere. I pulled into the Hilton because God wasn't ready to take my sorry ass.

The short Mexican lady at the front desk asked if I had a reservation; I told her no. Instead of paying $159 for the night, they charged $259 to my corporate American Express card. I took the white pass key with the Hilton logo emblazoned on one side and a magnetic strip on the other up to the room. The hotel cashier asked me if I knew how to use the keys. I smiled because I spent more time in hotel rooms than in my own bed. My rule of thumb was to never sleep in a woman's house unless she could give you the keys to the front door. A woman giving up the keys to the front door doesn't mean that she loves you or anything like that. It just makes the insanity plea work both ways. Like I said before, there are always rules to the game. I put my keys down on the small table in the hotel room next to the chair that I hung my jacket on. I picked up the remote next to the TV and lay down on the bed, my feet on the floor. I flipped through the stations, going from reality shows to dramas. The pay-per-view selections were of recent Hollywood duds. I settled on an Asian porno flick. I selected buy so that the $12.95 would be charged to my room. The first scene was two Asian women eating each other out in bed. After they had finished doing each other orally, the dildos came out.

"Fuck!" I turned the TV off and got up from the bed. I grabbed my jacket and headed out the door as if the smoke alarm had gone off in the room. I took the elevator and went to the first floor. The hotel bar was located to the left of the main lobby. I needed a drink like a motherfucker.

There were about ten people in the bar. Three middle-aged white men sat on bar stools, their wrinkled suits providing evidence of a long, exhausting day at the office. They each sat with a chair between them as if they were afraid of spreading their tiredness. There was a group of four young people sharing a pitcher of beer and Buffalo wings. NYC College of Technology logos were imprinted on their gray sweatshirts.

I ordered a Hoodlum and took it to a table with two chairs located three tables away from the college students. I was angrier with myself than Julie. Julie was my rock and my salvation. Life at home was becoming totally unbearable but I needed to stay put until I could leave for good. The Hoodlum tasted like the Hilton was following in the footsteps of Delta. In this case, the bartender had skimped on the alcohol. I thought about going back and asking for more alcohol but my butt felt like lead. The dramatics of the day were taking their toll on my body. It was the replay of my day that had taken me away from my reality. I didn't see when she came in and I was startled when she spoke.

"You look like the only one here who doesn't need to be carried to his room. Do you mind?" she asked, pointing to the chair opposite me.

"No," I said, looking at the blonde white woman pulling out the chair. She rested an apple martini on my table. She was dressed in a sheer white blouse with no bra, her perky breasts pointing at me. Her short denim mini-skirt disappeared under the table, allowing me only a fleeting glance at her legs.

"What's your story?" She wiggled herself in the chair as her eyes looked through me.

"Life and all its complications." The ice had melted in the drink, leaving me with water that tasted like unsweetened iced tea.

"My life is the opposite of complicated. I've been married for six years to my high school sweetheart. We have two children; Anthony, five, and Mary, two. This was supposed to be the weekend when we got the magic back in the big city." She stopped to take a sip of her drink. "Magic is the same as lust. Once it's gone, forget about it."

"Where's your husband now?" I asked, glancing over at the bar. I was still trying to decide if I was going to get another drink.

"He fell asleep, after he screwed me with his semi-erect penis," she said, looking directly into my eyes.

"Maybe you should've given him a blow job."

She laughed, as if I was about to replace Dave Chappelle.

"Look at me. I'm a white girl; our specialty is blowjobs. I sucked that man for half an hour to get his penis semi-erect. I stopped because I was getting dizzy from going up and down and his penis was starting to deflate."

I stared at her small, thin, pink lips. My dick had begun to itch. "So what do you want to do?"

"Aren't you the one from big bad New York City? What do you think I should do?" She continued to hold my gaze.

"We could go upstairs and fuck," I said.

"What would that do for me?" She bit into the slice of apple they had put in her martini.

"I'm not a psychiatrist. You implied that you were tired of semi-erect dick so I offered a hard one. You could take it or go upstairs to your husband." I pushed my drink away.

She picked up my glass and drank the remainder from her glass. "Life is complicated."

I watched as she walked to the bar. Her legs were long and well-toned. Her butt lifted up the skirt; making a nice indentation. I was going to fuck her.

"Hoodlum, you don't look like one," she said, placing the fresh drink in front of me. "You look more like a pretty boy."

This small talk was getting us off the topic. "Is your husband going to be up soon?"

"The hotel has to be on fire for my husband to wake up."

That was all I needed to hear. I put the glass to my mouth and finished the drink. She followed suit.

"What room are you in?" She pushed the chair back. I followed her action. "Room 224."

She smiled. "Maybe life is not that complicated after all."

I followed her up the stairs to my room. She leaned against the side of the wall, next to my door, while I slid the card in to unlock the door.

"What's so funny?" I asked.

"We're in room 220."

My dick became erect immediately. I grabbed her hand and rested it on the door knob. I came around behind her; lifting up her skirt. She didn't have on any panties. I slipped a condom onto my penis and I entered her immediately. I pounded into her fast and furious. As her decibels increased, I became even more excited. I was thinking about her husband, maybe asleep, maybe not, two doors down from us. It was giving me an erection that Viagra couldn't compete with. This was a good release from the tension of the day. I didn't know her last name and most likely I never would. We were two strangers reaching out for solace in a cruel world. Tomorrow belonged to no one right then. The sweat from my brow was dripping onto her pale butt. As I felt her body shiver, my scrotum started to itch and together we were about to collapse onto the floor. As we did, she let go of the door as if her hands were useless to her. I absorbed the force of the fall as I turned toward my right side and she fell on top of me. My penis lay flaccid against my leg as a door slammed outside. I got up off the floor, extending my hands out to her to lift her up. She clasped her hands around mine and, for the first time, I felt the warmth of her hand. I pulled the condom off and pulled up my pants as she adjusted herself.

"Can you open the bar and bring me one of the small bottles of Bacardi?" she asked.

As I went toward the small refrigerator, I sighed. I didn't need any more company for the night. "You want another drink this late?"

"No, but I need to do something."

I opened the cheap bottle of Bacardi and gave it to her.

"Thanks." She took the bottle and threw it down the front of her dress. The small remainder she drank quickly.

"Tricks of the trade?" I asked.

"No. Believe me or not, I've never cheated on my husband."

Normally I would've replied that Bush loved poor black people but I didn't.

"A girlfriend of mine told me about this. I have to go directly to the shower when I get in the room and I don't know what state my husband will be in when I get in. Now I don't care since I have every reason to go and take a shower. And God forbid he picks up my clothes, the smell will totally disgust him. You're a man so I'm sure you have some secrets."

"Yeah, I do, but this is a good one." I smiled.

"Thanks." She opened the door and poked her head outside.

"Maybe I'll see you again." I lied.

She looked back at me as if to say that I was dreaming. "No, it's time to go home forever. But thank you for everything."

I nodded and she walked out the door, closing it gently behind her.

After she left, I walked to the door and tested it to make sure that it was locked. I threw myself on the bed and night turned into day. The ringing of the cell phone jarred me awake and I stumbled toward the table. I picked it up and flipped it open. I didn't look at the number on the phone.

"Donald, get Emerald to school right now." The voice made me sit up on the bed, the events of the night becoming a distant memory.

"What?!" I exclaimed as the recognition of the voice came to me. "I am taking Emerald to school but we're not going back to the house."

Maybe a dial tone from a house phone would've made me realize that he wasn't on the phone anymore. With cell phones, it was different, a click and dead silence. I kept the phone to my ear, waiting to explain myself, but there was no one but me in the room. I looked at the time on the phone. It was 7:30 a.m. I grabbed my jacket and ran to the bathroom. I hung it on the bathroom doorknob as I quickly washed my face and brushed my teeth. I ran my hand through my hair and looked at myself in disgust as I opened the bathroom door. I picked up the bill that was slipped under the door and realized that they had already charged my card so there was no reason to stop at the front desk. I took the stairs two at a time and I was quickly in the parking lot. I clicked the car alarm and pulled the door open. I didn't get it more than halfway opened before it was slammed shut, the force almost taking my hand with the door. As I turned around, I barely saw the hand that ripped into my stomach, making me grasp for air. The second punch was even more vicious than the first. It dug into my ribs as I fell to the ground.

"Enough." The voice was the same one I had heard on the phone. I looked up to see the shiny, black, pointed shoe and gray head of my father-in-law, Mr. Malcolm. On either side of him were two big men; one Spanish and the other black. The black man, who looked like a rejected NFL line-backer, was rubbing his knuckles, eager to continue inflicting pain.

"Don't talk," Malcolm said as if I had the strength or desire to do that. "You know I hate repeating myself. Look at me, Donald. I'm an old man. I hate hurting people."

The two men snickered when he made that comment. He looked at them and they quickly clamped their mouths shut.

"I will call to talk to my grandson at home at six o'clock this evening. I would like for him to tell me how great school was and, besides being a little late because his father had an emergency, that everything was okay." Malcolm reached down and lifted me up to the car. "It's all right. You don't need to thank me for helping you up."

I watched them drive off in a tinted Lincoln sports car. I opened the trunk of the car and lifted the covering for the spare tire. The gun that the PI had given me lay between the tire and the wheel lug. I slammed the trunk down and pounded on it. Every dog has its day and I was sure that mine was coming. Today my name was John, but one day soon it would start with a P.

CHAPTER 5

"When did you stop seeing faces?" Donna asked, lying naked on the bed next to me. Her gray suit was folded neatly on the chair at the foot of the bed. We were at the Hilton on 42nd Street.

"A long time ago," I replied, understanding exactly what she meant. I couldn't recall ever talking to a girl with the intention of anything more than sex. Well, my wife was an exception. When I looked at her, I saw green. I had never been in love and the closest female friend I had was Julie.

"You are sad." Donna rocked her body on the bed.

"And you are better than me?" I asked, wondering what made her any different.

"You can't place me and you in the same class. At home is a husband whom I love dearly and it is reciprocated. I'm not perfect and I don't say that I am." She spoke in a monotone like Mrs. Silver, a boring history teacher I had in high school. She was merely stating facts and nothing but the facts. "If I wanted dick, I would be next to Brian right now, not you. You know the reason why we're here. This is business. The fact that we fuck is all good, but I'm not confused. Every man I have given this pussy to got it for a specific reason. They might get confused because it is so good but I never do."

The silky voice that made my loins tremble when I had first met her was gone. Unlike my experiences hundreds of times before, this was not about my looks. Even though her body was a million times better than my wife their interest in me was the same. "Your boss?"

"That's quite obvious. Without the white man getting a piece of my chocolate, we wouldn't be here right now. And do you know my salary? What secretary makes over seventy grand a year with perks? My husband and I get to go on vacation every year for free and I'm not talking about the Bahamas. Look at this pussy." Donna turned over and spread her legs. She was clean-shaven as usual. She took her fingers and parted the lips of her pussy, running her index fingers down the middle. Her eyes fluttered for a second as she laid her head on the pillow.

I had always maintained that I would not eat pussy and married pussy was definitely a no-no. Besides being the usual sperm bank reservoir for their husband, married women are always dangerous. Their lack of protection in dealing with their mate leaves you in a game of Russian roulette. I didn't know what Donna's husband was into and these days the propensity for the brothers to go in the wrong direction was suicidal. There might have been a reason why Donna had so much free time on her hands. She and her husband might've both been getting off, but maybe not with each other. I ran my hands up and down her legs all the way to her toes. She continued playing with her pussy, this time squeezing her pussy with one hand to expose her clit. She licked the finger on her other hand and started to rub her clit. We had finished having sex about an hour ago and my body was ready for another go-around. I reached down to lick her freshly pedicured toes.

"I see this is as far as you would go," Donna said, smiling.

My tongue traced down the sole of her feet.

"You are a freak."

"Yeah, I go where no other man has gone before." The tip of my tongue traced between her toes; then one by one, I took them in my mouth. Her body moved restlessly on the bed. A weekly pedicure appointment schedule and clean hygiene had left her feet looking and smelling deliciously clean. I had been with women that I would not even kiss but I would fuck them all night. Don't ask me why. Someone once said that on "any given Sunday," you would fuck almost anything. There are always Sundays in the week.

"You are insatiable," Donna whispered as her hands left her clit to take hold of her breasts.

"The last time you left much too early." I traced my tongue up the inside of her right leg. As my head lifted above her belly button, she held my head with her pussy-wet hands.

She gazed deeply into my eyes. "Fuck me."

I slid my condom-covered dick into her wet pussy and as she raked my back I pushed into her as hard as I could.

"Yes, fuck me hard. I want to feel you in my dreams." She wrapped her legs around my waist, clenching her teeth down on my right earlobe.

I pushed her back down on the bed and lifted her legs over my shoulders for maximum penetration, lifting her sweet butt as I drove into her. I had experienced good pussy before, but Donna's was excellent. I could understand a man falling in love over her pussy and I felt sorry for him. Her white boss had fallen for some sweet black pussy. Most men who have been with a few women would tell you that vagina wetness ranges from dry to a fucking river. Donna was in the perfect middle. And while she wasn't tight, her clasp was indeed God's gift to man.

I stopped and turned her over. I was stuck in awe. In front of me was a perfectly rounded ass. I hesitated for a second before I slowly eased myself into her. With every inch inserted, there was an 'ah' until my thighs collided with perfection, drawing me even deeper inside. It didn't take long until I realized that I was a mere mortal. I collapsed quickly behind the great wonder of humanity. I was a spent and broken man.

"Donald, can you hand me the plastic bag next to my hand bag? Donna said as if nothing had just happened. She was the consummate business-woman.

With great labor, I rose off the bed, feeling the effects of not being an eighteen-year-old man. Two orgasms for a man in his thirties were all she wrote. There are men who could tell you that they could go all night, but most will explain the pointlessness of it all. To not know a beautiful woman is to love her, but knowledge always comes with understanding. I understood Donna; therefore love was nonexistent.

I brought the bag back and threw it beside her.

Donna almost jumped off the bed. "Be careful."

"Why? What's in there?" I picked up on the concern in her voice.

She lifted the bag that had settled next to the white pillow. She reached into it and pulled out a long, slim, surgical knife. The eight-inch blade was sharpened on either side. She held the knife in her hand and twirled it around.

"What's that for?"

"Kathleen wants you to use it in the robbery," Donna said, continuing to play with the blade of the knife.

"Hold the fuck up. What do you mean, she wants me to use it in the robbery?"

"Relax, Donald. Let me explain." Donna sounded like a schoolteacher repeating something to a hard-headed kid.

"What do you mean by that?" I was getting pissed.

"That white bitch is not in this robbery for money. Her intention is to make certain that her husband never leaves her. And the only way she knows how to do that is to cripple the motherfucker. Now here is the fucking knife." Donna handed me the knife.

"Cripple!" I looked at her in disbelief. "I'm not crippling anyone. I don't like white people, but that doesn't mean I'm about to go around killing them. All I want is some money to take care of my business."

"Donald, this is no ordinary two-dollar holdup. We're talking about twenty million dollars. Now I would cut your balls off for that kind of money so take it easy and listen."

I grabbed a chair and dragged it to the foot of the bed. Donna was the one in charge and the quicker I understood that the better I would be able to play the game. At that point, I was the triggerman and she was the mob captain. But fuck if I was going to stay the triggerman. "All right, enlighten me."

"Kathleen doesn't want you to stab her husband. You think she trusts a black man to do that to her husband. You might kill the bastard and that will take this thing to another level."

"Now I'm totally lost. I guess four years of engineering is not helping me here," I said to Donna.

"Kathleen was one year away from graduating from med school when she met Peter, her husband. At that time, she was also dating a surgeon. The surgeon had just graduated from med school. The surgeon was making money but not enough to buy Kathleen a brand-new Porsche. After a continent-hopping romance, Kathleen and Peter got married. From there, they tried the pregnancy thing, but Peter was shooting blanks and Kathleen didn't want any of the other procedures."

I put my hand over my mouth and pretended to yawn. While Kathleen's story was interesting, I didn't have time for it.

"I get the hint," Donna said to me. "The point is that Kathleen will stab her husband. You're merely carrying the knife to her. Donald, you don't have to do much for the twenty million dollars we're splitting. Kathleen and I planned this thing down to the smallest detail. All you have to do is to use the key that I'll give you later to unlock the handcuffs. You then have to take a blowtorch and burn around his wrists to make it look like the handcuffs were chipped off his hands. Timing is the most important factor. You will only have fifteen seconds to knock Peter out, wait for Kathleen to stab Peter, then punch her in her face. You have to hit her hard; make sure she loses a tooth or two."

"Wait, Donna. Kathleen wants me to hit her in her face so hard that she might even lose teeth?" I shook my head. "Women never want you to touch their faces."

"Donald, you don't understand the stakes here. Kathleen gave up her whole life for this man. A little reconstructive surgery means nothing to her. There can't be even a hint that she was involved with this. She needs to be immediately eliminated as a suspect." Donna rummaged through the bag and came out with a pair of women's gloves. She handed them to me. "You'll give her these gloves; then she'll give them back to you after she stabs her husband."

"I guess I have to wear a good mask," I said, happy to know that I didn't have to kill anyone.

"No mask involved. You put on a mask and it draws a lot of attention. I'll give you another suitcase." Donna knelt down on the bed and lifted my head with her hands. She moved my face from side to side. "You'll be wearing a nice blonde wig. You'll just be another handsome white man going home from work."

"You think that I could pass for a blond white man?"

Donna looked at me over and over. "Yep, they won't even say a light-skinned or Hispanic man. Nope, they will label you a handsome blond."

I got up and went to look at myself in the bathroom mirror. I had never thought of passing myself off as a white man before but Donna was right. Once I lost the curly hair that hinted at my Negro blood, I would be all White.

I walked back into the room. "You are right."

"Donald, you haven't told anyone about this, have you?" Donna's eyes were unwavering as they latched onto mine.

"No," I lied, giving her back the same stare. I had learned to lie at an early age. Once an older sister of a girl I was seeing taught me how to do it. As we lay in her bed next to her sister, my girlfriend's bed, she asked me what I would say if my girlfriend asked me if I would sleep with her sister. I turned to her and looked her directly in the eyes and I said, "I would say no." She laughed at me. She told me that her sister would know instantly that I was lying. I asked her how she would be able to tell. I didn't blink nor did I move any other part of my body. She told me the human body had thousands of veins in it and she pointed at my dick. Some you cannot control but others you can. That day she taught me how to control every nerve in my body. Our affair didn't last too long after that because while we could lie like politicians, we couldn't control our lust. One day her sister caught us fucking in her bed.

"Good. Because the number one reason people get caught is because they can't keep their fucking mouths shut. Sink or swim, you, me and Kathleen have everything riding on this. I've always wanted to open a boutique and maybe this will give me the chance to do it." Donna got off the bed.

"A boutique? You don't need ten million dollars to open a boutique."

"When you are doing it on Fashion Avenue in Manhattan you do. I don't want any little small ass boutique on Flatbush Avenue. People coming and ask you to take something off of the $9.95 retail price. In my boutique, a lace will cost a buck fifty."

"Why don't you just advertise that you've just robbed your boss of twenty million dollars because everyone will know?"

"Donald, do I look stupid to you? I don't think you would be in this room right now if you believed that," Donna said, putting sweatpants over her spectacular ass. "I will be managing the store, my brother. I'll only be a manager. The store will be owned by a real estate developer with millions of dollars."

"I'm sure you already have someone in mind."

Donna smiled. "I paid cash for the room so, as always, you can stay the night or go home. I'm sure you'll be spending the night." Donna pulled the hotel room door open. I slumped down onto the bed, the knife wrapped in the plastic bag in one hand and the gloves in the other.

The Japanese sushi chef used a long knife to cut the salmon into one-inch pieces, then wrapped it around white flaky dough. He sprinkled a few things over it, then poured a sauce in a small bowl and laid it down in front of Julie.

"Doesn't this look beautiful?" she asked.

I waited for the waiter to arrive with my Shrimp Tempura rolls. After he placed the plate in front of me, I stretched my hands out, palms up, presenting the rolls to Julie.

"Now that's food." I used chopsticks, picked up a slice of the roll and dipped it into the sauce. I savored the taste of the shrimp combined with the other unknown ingredients. I chased that down with some hot tea.

"There's nothing like salmon sushi." Julie devoured the last of her very pink sushi. Her facial expression mimicked that of Tyra Banks' in an explosion of joy as she welcomed one of her guests. "You were saying that Donna gets ten million dollars. Why does that bitch have to get half, when you're taking all the risks?"

"Donna was the one who set up the entire deal. Either way, I walk away a wealthy man."

"Five million maybe, but not ten million." There was a serious tone in Julie's voice that was totally unexpected. The fact that I was actually sitting down and talking to her about the robbery was totally unexpected; for that matter. Initially, when I had told her about it, she was totally against it until I told her the amount of money that was involved. Her change in direction was as swift as a fish swimming into the mouth of a shark. I was surprised but happy that she understood what I was doing and why I was doing it. She prodded me until I told her the complete plan and today I was about to update her on what Donna had told me yesterday.

"And you said that all this goes down in fifteen days?"

"Yes, starting from tomorrow."

"Who will pick you up after the robbery?"

I looked around the room. The nearest table was about fifteen feet away and Julie was talking in a very low voice. "Can you stop repeating robbery?"

"Yeah, you're right. We have to be more careful."

"We? Since when are you a part of this?"

Julie held my hands and looked me straight in the eyes. "Donald, you are about to rob a man of twenty million dollars and your partners are two women. Women are the most vicious and evil things that God ever made. There are only two people who could think like a woman; another woman or God. And guess what? God is not an option."

Her hands felt gentle and warm and her words wrapped around me like a warm blanket on a chilly morning. Her hair, combed with a bang at the side of her left eye, gave her an angelic appearance. As I squeezed her hand, I realized that my body was sliding into hers.

She quickly jerked her hand away from mine as if sensing our intermingling spirits. "We are not gonna go there."

"Go where?" I asked innocently. "Do you want to go to the ball game this weekend with me and Emerald?"

"No, sorry; Brian and I are going to the Poconos."

She shot the knife right through my chest. I didn't want to hear that now. "Oh, I forgot to ask how you and Brian are doing."

"It's been great. We're having a ball. Brian's a really good guy. I think he might propose to me over the weekend." She motioned the waiter over.

Not only had she plunged the knife into my chest, she was now turning it.

"But you love the ball game," I said weakly, appealing to a time long gone.

"Yeah, but I love a honeymoon Jacuzzi suite much better than seeing men run around in tights. Even though Derek Jeter could relieve any sore eyes."

"Well, you'll have to explain it to Emerald. I already told him you were coming." I was desperate.

"Stop this right now, Donald. Do not let our friendship go down that road. You will explain to Emerald that I couldn't make it this weekend and I'll call him when I get back. I'll try to take him to the movies with Brian next weekend. There's a new animated movie opening up."

"Sorry, I didn't mean to do that, but lately we haven't really been spending time together."

This was the truth. I had really started to miss Julie; it seemed like she never had any time for me. The only time she seemed to be available was when we had to discuss the plans for the robbery.

"Donald, stop acting like a baby. I'm not going anywhere permanently. Let's talk some more about the upcoming event. I want to make sure you're protected. After the event, who picks you up?"

"Do you think Donna will let anyone but herself pick me up?"

"Nope, because that's when she'll try to hurt you. I guarantee you Donna will not be there by herself."

"There's no one else in on the plan. Who can she get to help her?"

Julie started to laugh. "Do you remember the first time you slept with Donna? You told me that she was the kind of woman that a man would kill for. Now ask yourself that same question over again."

"You've got me there. She doesn't even need to pay anyone. Just a promise would be enough to get someone to bust a cap in my ass."

"Now, do you understand why you need me? We've known each other for how many years? Are you going to trust Donna or me?"

I had never seen that kind of cunning in Julie and, as we sat down to map out the pickup, I was very happy that I had her on my side. I realized that I might have to blackmail Donna to keep more of the money but I was planning to be alive to do it. As Julie explained it, I would not have been alive.

"So what do you have in mind?"

Julie took a piece of a napkin and started to draw a map of the streets.

"Donna's expecting to pick you up here," she said, pointing to a dark alley-way where Donna was supposed to be waiting. "But you'll go in the opposite direction and a yellow cab will pick you up right here."

"What yellow cab?"

"Leave that to me. Donna has her ways and I have mine."

I couldn't picture Julie convincing a man to do anything. But I had been wrong before and, looking in Julie's eyes, I knew that no matter what she had to do, there was going to be a cab waiting to pick me up.

I took a deep breath and exhaled slowly. "I found my father."

Grandma gave me a brief glance, then continued to take the food out of the pot. "Is he alive?"

"Yes, he lives upstate in Albany." I sipped slowly at the red homemade sorrel drink.

"I wanted to kill him, you know." She made the statement apologetically. "But I couldn't. If I had done that, there would have been no one to take care of you."

"How did you know who he was?" I asked. "It cost me a pretty penny to find him."

"At that time, there was a brief trial but, of course, no one was found guilty. Three men had been accused. I didn't care who I killed. I just wanted to kill one of them." As she spoke, the pain was evident in the tightening of her voice. She brought the food and placed it in front of me.

"Grandma, you're not going to eat?" She had just finished cooking when I walked into the house.

"No, Son, my stomach is filled up with emptiness." Tears started to fall from her eyes as she held onto the top of the chair. "I can't eat a thing."

I quickly got up and sat her down on a chair before returning to mine. "Don't worry, Mom. I'll take care of everything."

"Donald, don't go and do anything stupid. Remember, you have your son to think about."

"I know, Mom. I merely plan to talk to him. I want him to know that I'm alive."

I had stopped eating to look at my grandmother. I could see that I had brought up some terrible memories. She shook her head profusely and kept wringing her hands.

"He killed my only daughter." Grandma stared up at the picture of my mother. "For years, there has been an emptiness in my heart because of it. You helped a lot, but I sometimes miss your mother so much that I still cry to this very day."

I rose and placed my hands around my grandmother's shoulders, tapping her ever so gently. Inside my heart, a rage was building against my father. In creating me, he had destroyed so much. I'm sure that once my mom had left the penitentiary, he must have gone back to life as usual. I clenched my fists to hold back the tears I now wished to share with my grandmother. I also clenched my fists because I wanted to kill my father. I didn't know him and I hated his presence on this earth.

My grandmother took some deep breaths and wiped the tears away from her eyes. "Forgive me, Son."

"Mom, stop it. There isn't anything to forgive you for."

I pulled my chair closer to her and held her hand, as time slowly ticked away. Besides my son, my grandmother was the only family I had left. She had given me so much and whatever I had done for her was never enough. I had planned a trip to upstate Albany the following day with hopes of finding some kind of resolution. I had always wanted to find my father, but not for a tear-jerking Oprah reunion. I wanted to find him and punish him for bringing me into the world the way that he did. He had destroyed in order to create, then walked away from his creation. I wasn't the product of a sailor or a priest; I was the product of a rapist. It was a label that I carried in my heart throughout my life; unbeknownst to the people around me. Julie was the only person who knew my true origin.

"No, Emerald, Julie isn't coming with us today," I said as we pulled out of the driveway.

It was a hard lesson, but Emerald had come to realize that his mother and

I would not be attending too many events together. Except for special occasions, like birthdays or gathering at his grandparents' house, he would either be with me and Julie or only me. I hated the occasions when Lauren and Annette took my son but, as with many things in my life, at present I couldn't do a damn thing about it. There were no fucking two mommies in Emerald's life. There was a mommy, a daddy and a thing. A woman acting and dressing like a man, but not a man; even if she hit like one.

"Daddy, do you know how they make animated films?" Emerald was the first one out of the car. He waited as I secured the vehicle opposite a pizza restaurant on Court Street.

I clasped his hand in mine. "I assume that they're made with computers, Emerald."

"Daddy, you're silly. It's a lot more involved than that." He giggled in delight of his knowledge as we walked across Court Street.

"Well, tell me what's involved in making animated movies."

"Okay." A big smile spread over his face. As we rode up to the movie theater, Emerald explained the animation process to me to the amazement of the people in the elevator. At the end of the ride, a white, middle-aged woman, with a boy about eight years old, stopped us as we were getting off.

"I hate to be rude, but how old is your son?" she asked.

"He's four," I said.

She was astounded. "No kidding? My son can barely read the menu in a restaurant and your son gave us a lesson in animation."

There wasn't anything else I could say. Emerald was advanced for his age. He tugged on my arm for us to go, looking at the watch on his hand.

"Enjoy the movie," I said as I left with Emerald in tow.

Emerald opened the front door and ran upstairs to his bedroom. He already knew the regimen of changing his clothes and brushing his teeth. He also knew never to go into his mother's room unless she told him to come in. It was a rule implemented by Annette, who seemed to run the house.

Annette had also put a lock on the master bedroom door, which she utilized constantly. My son's bathroom was adjoining his bedroom. Therefore, there was no need for him to enter the master bathroom. The door to my room was always open so he could come in and out as he pleased. I did very little but sleep in there so there was no need to put a lock on my door. The bathroom for the guestroom that I used was small. It held a shower with no tub, a commode and a washbasin with a mirror. There were two maids who came in twice a week to clean the house.

As my son was running up the steps, he was met by his mother, who kissed him good night and promised to come and read him a bedtime story. She continued down the stairs as I made my way toward the refrigerator.

I had flipped open a bottle of Heineken and taken a long swig when I encountered Lauren.

"How was the movie?" Her robe was open, exposing her bra and panties. She looked like Dracula's bride before she was fed.

I grunted. I neither felt like seeing her body nor engaging in any pathetic conversation.

"Donald, you know the situation we're in. You're not going anywhere and I'm not going anywhere. The sooner you come to that realization, the better things will be. We can be a normal family."

She went over to the electric kettle, filled it up with water and turned it on.

"*Normal!*" I was heated. "This shit could never be normal. Like Kunta Kinte in *Roots*, I'll always run away from this shit. You're fucking crazy; talking about normal. If you look around, you'll see that there isn't a single normal aspect of our life. That bitch upstairs uses you as her punching bag. Emerald can't come into your room and you have to come up with all these lame excuses why your eyes are bruised or your lips are swollen. Wake up; this is not fucking *normal*."

Lauren calmly poured the hot water over the tea bag in the cup. "And what you do is better than my situation? Putting your dick into each and every pussy you find is normal? I'm surprised that your dick hasn't fallen clear off yet. If you die from AIDS, what will become of your precious son? If you love him and you want to save him from all this evil, don't you think your behavior should change? Do you think that you would be any different if I wasn't a lesbian? Hell to the naw! You would still be doing what you're doing. You bastard; you're sicker than me. You always have been."

"I doubt that," I said, finishing up the beer. "Emerald is the only reason I'm here. Every night I pray that our brilliant kid doesn't get fucked up in the head because of our situation. He doesn't deserve this."

"Oh, and you think that if you take him out of this house and go out on your own with him he will be better off? Donald, you've got issues too. Just because your mother killed herself after your birth, you feel entitled to do what you do."

I was stunned as I got up from the island. "I never told you about my mother."

"You didn't have to tell me. My father knew everything about you before I took my wedding vows."

"What does my mother's incident have to do with this?"

"Nothing, Donald, it means nothing at all. But the fact that you think that somehow you are in a better situation than me is ridiculous. You will be right next to me burning in hell."

I dumped the empty bottle into the garbage can. "To be honest with you, I don't know if my son living with me will be the best thing for him. What I'm certain of is that I refuse to let him grow up in this house with you and your whatever the fuck you want to call her. For as long as I'm able to breathe, I will try to get him out of this house. Your other choice is to get that bitch out. You might need her, but Emerald doesn't."

"Annette stays and, as we all know, you're not going anywhere. My father will never allow you to leave with Emerald and, without him, you're going nowhere. So go to your room, reach into the cooler and drink yourself to sleep, like you do every night." She sounded like a mother sending a disobedient child to bed.

The gust of wind from her robe was the only indication that she had left. A minute later, I heard the door to the master bedroom slam.

I walked slowly up the stairs. Lauren was certain that I had no choice but to endure this living. In the room, I reached into the cooler and took out another Heineken. I went into the closet and unlocked the safe. I took the gun out and checked for the bullets in the magazine. I returned the magazine to the chamber. I took the gun and walked toward my bed. I sat down on the bed, my head drooped low, the gun in my right hand.

The bar was cloudy, not like most dimly lit bars. This one had gray smoke coming from the floor. I wondered if they had recently installed a smoking gadget to attract new customers. Judging from the number of customers in there at the present moment, they definitely needed to try something else. The smoking gadget wasn't working. The bartender had brought my drink and disappeared into the back. Hennessy on the rocks guaranteed to increase your blood pressure. In other words, the black man killer drink. I tried to look at the time on my watch but the smoke was too much, so I gave up and picked up my drink once more. She had chosen the bar so I could only wait for her arrival. It wasn't clear to me if I was hungry or simply nervous. My stomach had begun to boil to indicate an abnormality in my being. I had called her because I desperately needed someone to talk to. I couldn't ever remember a time when I needed her so much. She needed to be there for me; I needed to look at her and explain my predicament.

"Hello, Donald," she said as she sat down next to me.

I looked over at her. As always, I was awestruck by her beauty. Her face was a perfect photograph. Her smile was a content one that made the viewer certain that she was confident in her appearance.

"Hi, Mom," I said.

"You seem troubled, Donald. Is there anything your mother can do?" she asked.

"Would you like a drink?" I asked, hoping the bartender would reappear. I hadn't seen him since he had poured me that first drink. It wasn't that I wanted a refill or anything like that. My drink seemed to have stayed the same since he had poured it; even the ice cubes seemed not to have melted.

"Mama didn't tell you? Your mother never drank. I'm never thirsty. How's

Mama doing? I hope she's doing well. She's a very good woman. One day I'll have to sit down with her and talk. I'm sure a lot has happened since I left. She'll tell me all the bad things you did, Donald. I hope you've been a good boy."

My mother lifted her hand and ran her fingers through my hair. I felt a cool breeze rifling through my curly hair.

"Mom, I found Daddy," I said, looking at her for an immediate reaction.

She looked a little puzzled. "So, how do you know that he's your father?"

"I'm ninety-nine-point-nine percent positive that it's him."

"I don't know what to say, Donald. I never knew your father too well. Except for him ordering me around, I never really spoke to him. Because of what he did to me, I know he's an evil man, but that's about it. What are you going to do with him?"

She had asked the question I didn't know the answer to. "I don't know," I said, certain she could read my mind.

"When are you going to see him?"

"Tomorrow morning."

"Where?"

"I heard he likes hunting and tomorrow is supposed to be a big deer hunting day. People come from all over the country to hunt in upstate New York."

"You got a gun?"

"Yeah, I bought one."

"Are you going to use it?"

"I don't know; I was hoping you could tell me what to do."

"Animals are tough to kill and sometimes killing them could cause more harm than good. They sometimes fight back and you can also get hurt. You have to think about what you have to lose."

"Mom, I thought about it. I lost you."

"Boy, that was a long time ago. Don't do it for me; I'm sure you have other people that you need to protect."

I held the glass in my hand as tears ran down my eyes. "Mom, someone has to pay for what they did to us. We can't let him get away with it. Someone's got to pay."

Again the cool breeze ran through my hair and my shoulders felt cold.

"It's okay, Son. Everything will work itself out. It's okay."

The loud knocking on the door jolted me awake. I looked at the door and wondered why it was locked. I always kept my door unlocked just in case my son needed to come in. As I got off the bed, the gun fell from my hand onto the floor. Slowly, realization of my actions came back to me. I had gotten up and locked the door after I had removed the gun from the safe. I quickly returned the gun to the safe and wiped the sweat off my face. I looked over at the clock. It was 9:00 p.m. I must have dozed off.

I opened the door and my son came in.

"Hi, Daddy."

"What are you still doing up, Emerald?"

"Daddy, why was the door locked?"

"I must've locked it by accident. I'm sorry, Son."

"Daddy, can you take me to school in the morning?"

"No, Emerald, I have to leave to go on some business later tonight."

Emerald's face looked sad. "I wanted you to take me to school."

"I'm sorry. I promise that I will take you to school the day after tomorrow."

I felt terrible, disappointing my son, but I had to take care of business.

"You promise."

"I do. Now come give your dad a kiss and I will see you tomorrow."

After my son left I started to get ready for my trip to upstate New York. I was going hunting. The FedEx package Donna had sent to me was on the table in my room. I hadn't opened it, because I knew it contained the wig that I was to use in the robbery. Donna had said she would order it and I would pick it up from her. I wondered what had made her change her mind on the procedure. She had obviously ordered it and sent it directly to me. Could this be a ploy on her part? I took the package and tossed it into the back of the Hummer. I had already hidden the gun under the spare tire. I was dealing with the root of all evil; yet my time to contemplate various actions was limited. The wig had arrived at a perfect time. It gave me an opportunity to prove Donna's theory. Tomorrow morning, I was going to be a blond white man.

CHAPTER 7
14TH DAY

I was glad I didn't drink any more Heinekens because the trip upstate was going to take at least two hours. The only good thing was that I was leaving at night, therefore the traffic should be very light. From the FDR I was going to jump onto the George Washington Bridge to the Palisades Parkway onto the 87 thruway and head toward upstate New York. Fisher's Hunting Park was approximately two hours away from New York City. Even though the Hummer averaged less than ten miles per gallon, the large capacity of the tank made it possible to drive for hours without refueling.

At 10:00 p.m., I got off the Palisades at a rest stop ten minutes from the George Washington Bridge. There was only one other car parked about ten car lengths from me. I waited fifteen minutes for the other car to leave. Even though the Hummer was a few feet above the ground, the windows weren't tinted; therefore anyone could look in. And even though New Yorkers wouldn't come to your rescue if a crime was being committed, they were very curious people. I walked to the back of the truck, opened it and pulled out the package. I looked over at incoming traffic and saw a car's right signal light on. I quickly got back into the car and waited. The green Honda Accord seemed to have changed its mind and kept going with its right signal light still on. I sat down in the passenger side, a nervous wreck. I hadn't done anything wrong; yet my forehead was sweating profusely. I placed the black fitted stockings over my head, using my right hand to secure my hair underneath. I then slipped the blond wig over my head and adjusted it while looking in the mirror.

The transformation was immediate. The person looking back at me was no longer a light-skinned black man but a white man. I quickly discarded the box in a garbage bin that was filled with McDonald's and Burger King bags. I walked confidently back around the truck and climbed into the driver's seat. I looked into my rear view mirror and pulled out of the scenic rest stop. I changed the radio station to CD 101.9 and settled in for the ride to Fisher's Hunting Park.

As the city, with its smog and human congestion lay behind me, I was feeling good about the openness of the suburbs. Houses were no longer yards apart but often as much as a mile. Most tourists had never heard about these suburbs, where white picket fences and cows and pigs are a common part of everyday life. No, they preferred to think of New York as a congested and polluted place, where people would rather shoot you than say good morning. I cracked the window to take in some of the freshness of the outdoors; knowing that as fast as I was leaving, I would be returning to the city of my birth. In the back of the car were a hunting bag, raincoat and dark sunglasses. The clouds, followed by a light drizzle, had made the night darker than usual.

I had made a decision to confront my father. I wanted him to tell me why my entrance to this earth had to be under such dire circumstances. It was odd but I had not missed my father even once while growing up. I had never cried out for him, even though many of my friends and classmates would talk about their fathers. Maybe it was because there were so many other kids in the same boat as me. We did not have fathers but the mothers and grandparents who raised us were doing a phenomenal job. A single-parent household usually meant one available parent whereas I had none. I'm not sure if it was the way that my mom exited the earth that caused me to want her so much, or if it was her picture that stood on my grandma's wall that kept knocking in my head. I needed my mother to be with me in the worst way.

The hours went by as the Hummer boomed its way upstate. I pulled into the Seek Motel, located about two miles away from Fisher's. The meeting with my father could turn ugly so I was taking all the necessary precautions, just in case. As advertised, the motel was cheap with no amenities. An elderly black man sat behind the front desk.

"Good afternoon," I said, walking up to him.

"Forty dollars a night, and no loud music or cussing. You're welcome to bring as many people into the room as you like, but there's only hot water for two showers a day. There are sheets and towels in the closet for a week. No maid service and checkout is at one." He turned his attention back to watching a small, outdated white television set with a blurry picture.

I reached into my pocket. "Okay."

"No credit cards," he said, not taking his eyes off the TV. "And you pay each day."

I took out my wallet and laid two crisp twenty-dollar bills on the counter.

"What's your name, Boy?" the old man said, getting up from his chair. "Not too many white men with good teeth rent rooms here. Are you trying to fool around on the Mrs.?"

"Not at all. It seems like all the other hotels around here are booked. Is there something happening in town today?"

"I guess you're really not from these parts. Today's the start of the hunting season. Fisher's Hunting Park is a couple of miles from here. They gonna have a good season, seeing as all the big hotel rooms are sold out."

I held my hand out for the keys. He slammed them down on the counter.

"Thank you." I picked up the two rusty silver keys with the number ten on the keychain.

"I should raise the price. Wherever there is one white guy, another one is sure to follow. Have yourself a good night. I'll be here in the morning. It's sixty dollars for tomorrow."

"Bastard," I whispered loud enough for him to hear.

"White people; they want it all for themselves," he said as I pulled the door shut.

The hotel room was surprisingly clean for the price. However, the walls were painted a hideous brown color and the drawings of airplanes adorning the ceiling did nothing to enlighten the room. The small, blue closet on the side of the bed contained five wire hangers, towels and a set of white sheets. I put my overnight bag on the only chair in the room. I went into the bathroom that consisted of a standup shower and a washbasin with a small oval mirror above it. Next to the washbasin was an unopened bar of Irish Spring soap. I opened it and washed my hands. There were no towels in the bathroom; therefore I had to walk back into the bedroom to retrieve a small towel from the closet. There was a "Not Working" sign on top of the 19-inch TV located at the foot of the bed. I pushed it to the side of the room and sat down on the bed. I took the folder that Bill had given me out of the bag. It contained a complete rundown on the hunting event. There was a large club area where most of the hunters hung out before heading out into the woods. He suggested that I approach my father at the event. Apparently, he was quite the talker, so getting his attention should be easy. I took the picture of my father, sitting at a bar with a Budweiser in his hand, out of the folder and slipped it into my shirt pocket.

The rain had subsided as I drove to the hunter's meeting place. I parked my truck in a lot filled with pickup trucks, SUV's and vans. I parked the Hummer behind a pickup truck that had a bumper sticker which read, "I hunt for my food." I laughed. I didn't think there was anyone in America who hunted for food. Steal and kill for food but never hunt. Most of these so-called hunters had paid exorbitant amounts of money for their hunting equipment. A deer or two would never be enough to cover such costs. I had paid about four hundred dollars for my camouflage outfit, boots and shoulder bag; probably a third of the rest of them.

"You ready, Son?" The voice came from an old man sitting in the passenger side of a pickup truck. The door was open and the man was cleaning a brown rifle with a telescopic sight at the top.

"Yeah, been waiting for this all year." I tried to sound convincing, but did not know what else to say.

"Me too, my friend. It's going to be a good year. So, what you carrying?" He looked through the sights of the gun.

My cell phone rang at the same time that I was trying to fabricate a response. I breathed a sigh of relief. "Got to go."

The old man grunted and continued inspecting his rifle.

I looked down at the phone number. It was Brian. I hadn't told Brian about this trip and I wasn't about to now.

"What's up, Brian?" I continued walking toward the restaurant.

"I'm in love!"

I pulled the phone away from my ear. His excitement had created a high pitch in his voice. I had never heard Brian so excited. He had spoken to me about women before but never like this. This was a new Brian.

I asked the dumbest question in the world. "With whom?"

"Who do you think?"

I stopped and leaned on the hood of a black Chevy Impala.

"Julie." I prayed that he would name someone else.

"Yes."

His answer had been expected, but still, I was disappointed. My last meeting with Julie had been an eye opener. I had crossed the boundary that friends are not supposed to cross. I had swum across the alligator-infested lake ready to battle the lion, naked except for a six-inch knife between my teeth.

"Are you sure?" I asked, reaching deeper into my soul.

"We spent the weekend together and I have never felt like this about a woman."

The words coming from the phone made my hands shake. Brian had taken my virgin. He had taken the woman who I had placed on that pedestal.

"That's great." I said, half-heartedly. I had major plans for Julie. Didn't she feel what I felt when I touched her hand?

"Man, everything is coming together for me. How many more days before we do that thing?" he asked.

"Fourteen." I pushed myself off the Impala and walked down the stairs to the restaurant. "Got to go, Brian."

I opened the door to what seemed more like a high school cafeteria than a restaurant. Two hundred or so men and women had gathered for the event. Women's rights had come a long way; they were delighted to kill animals too.

"Find a seat; we'll find you," a young white woman, not a day over twenty-one, advised me as she bustled past me in a tight white T-shirt and a pair of khaki shorts. My eyes scanned the room for the man whose face matched the picture in my pocket. Bill had instructed me to follow the alcohol but, in this setting, that was of absolutely no help.

"How you doing, big fellow?" a white, middle-aged woman asked as I started to walk to the bar.

She wasn't much to look at, with a big gut and gigantic breasts. She was sitting at a small table with an extra chair. There was a pitcher of beer and a plate with a burger and fries on it.

"Good. You want company?" I asked, still searching the room for my father.

"Yeah, why not? My girlfriend's supposed to meet me here but her husband didn't get in yet." She pushed the empty chair out with her foot.

I extended my hand to her. "I'm Peter."

"Marge." She gripped my hand tightly and shook it up and down.

I divided the room into quadrants; searching for my father. "It's really crowded in here."

"This must be your first time here," Marge said, filling her mouth with the yellow liquid in her glass. "You want a glass?"

"Sure. I guess it's going to be a while before the waitress comes back."

"At least twenty to thirty minutes. It took them about an hour to get me this burger and this shit's medium rare." She pointed at the redness in the middle of the burger. "You here by yourself?"

"Just like you, my friends couldn't make it."

"And the wife?"

"Never had that."

"Is that a good or a bad thing?"

I smiled at her. "Today it's a very good thing."

She started to blush; her face becoming blotchy red. Her short blonde hair was curled tightly over her ears. I wasn't looking at Marge as a woman; she was going to be an excuse. As always, I carried my Viagra pills, so getting turned on wasn't an issue. I smiled inwardly because life had come full circle; men could now fake it as much as women. How can you doubt a man when his erection is staring you straight in your face?

I rose. "I'll go get me a glass."

"Bring back some ice. This beer's been sitting here for a while."

There was a whole lot of stop-and-go traffic to the bar. I tried to make it there without ending up on a table or pushing someone else on one. I was a few feet away from the bar when I spotted him. He was sitting next to another man, about the same age as him. He had turned around briefly to talk to the man.

My world had stopped for a brief moment. I didn't know whether I should advance or retreat. He was laughing, a full set of white teeth testifying to his mood. I had to take a chance. I turned back and hurried to Marge.

"You're back. I thought one of the young waitresses had picked you up."

"No, but I have to run. One of my buddies is waiting for me at the bar." I picked up my knapsack.

"Oh." The disappointment was evident in her voice. "I guess I'll see you around."

"No, not if I don't have your cell phone number. Are you staying around here?" I took out my phone and entered her name.

"Yeah, my hotel is behind the restaurant." She perked up; straightening her rain-dampened clothing. "I met a few people earlier. Maybe I'll go hunting with them. Then again, I might stay in my hotel room. Here's my number."

I kept looking toward the bar as I entered her phone number in my phone. "I'll call you later."

I turned and started to walk back toward my father, and my date with destiny. I walked up to the bar area directly opposite from him. I squeezed between two middle-aged white men. I motioned for the bartender and he acknowledged me. I doubted that he would be getting to me anytime soon.

My father and the other man seemed to be having an intense conversation. I was curious to know what they were discussing, but I didn't want my father to become suspicious. As in the picture, real life had been hard on him. The lines on his face were sharp and his eyes hadn't stood up to the test of time. They were yellow and dull.

The man my father was talking to shouted at him, then left. I found a spot around the bar opposite from my father and nudged into a seat. The bartender came over to me and I ordered a drink. It was a drink I would nurse for the next few hours. Finally I watched my father finish his ninth drink before putting some money on the bar. By the time he turned around, I was a few inches away from him. He pushed people aside as he stormed out. I followed him, doing the same so as not to lose sight of him. I trailed him to a blue pickup that looked practically as old as him. There were dents and rust spots all over it. A "Retired Corrections Officer" sticker adorned the bumper. My father opened the truck and pulled out a big, long, black bag. He slung it over his shoulder. It was 5:25 a.m.

My father looked around and started down a dirt road. I was stuck; I didn't know what to do. I couldn't follow him without creating suspicion. Yet, this in itself was a great opportunity. Instead of being in the woods with hundreds of people, it would be just my father and me. I waited until I could see my father a good distance away; then I took the same path. I walked quickly, making sure that I didn't lose my visual on the man in camouflage ahead of me. In my hunting knapsack I had a long piece of stick to imitate a hunting rifle. It was my feeble way of trying to fit in with people I had nothing in common with.

"Hold it there, young man." I stopped dead in my tracks and looked around, trying to find out where the voice had come from.

"What?" I was surprised. Even though I had never heard my father's voice, I was one hundred percent positive that it was his.

"Come over here." There was a certain amount of authority in the voice.

"Where?" I asked, turning around in circles, trying to find the direction where the voice was coming from.

"Over here." I swung around once more and my father was pointing a high-powered rifle at me. He had a silly smirk on his face as if he had just caught me dipping in the cookie jar.

"What's this all about?" I asked.

"Well, for starters, you're not a hunter. You've been following me since the restaurant. Now I've been in law enforcement for decades and I have a lot of enemies; most of them good-for-nothing Niggers. But you, I've never seen you before. The only reason I didn't shoot you is because you remind me of my son. He wouldn't be caught dead out here though; he's a big-city lawyer." My father stopped and lowered the gun. "What do you want?"

"I heard that you're the best hunter out here. I was hoping you could teach me a thing or two. This is my first time."

"This being your first time is quite obvious, but you trying to learn to hunt don't sit right with me. You could've approached me at the restaurant."

"You were involved in a heated conversation in the restaurant. I didn't want to interrupt." I was hoping the third degree would finish soon.

"What's your name, Son?" my father asked.

"Peter. And yours?"

"Jim. I retired from corrections five years ago," he stated proudly.

"Where's the best place to hunt around here?" I asked, hoping to get us walking again.

"Well, Son, if you have it in you, let's go. I usually hunt alone but I guess there's nothing wrong with someone tagging along." My father turned around and headed into the bushes. "I'm too old to change diapers so either you keep up or you get left behind."

"Don't worry about me. I'll be right behind you every step of the way."

I pulled the bag tightly over my shoulder and followed my father's footsteps. I was concerned about our introduction but, as always in life, things take care of themselves. I thought I was going to hate my father, but it wasn't working out that way. Jim seemed like an old man who was happy to be alive, doing what he wanted to do. Yes, my father was an ordinary white man.

The trek through the bushes was long and painful. My father led the way with grunts and minor conversation about the other hunters. After about forty-five minutes of fast walking, we stopped in a heavily wooded area with a clearing in the middle.

"Now we sit and wait. You can take out your rifle now," Jim said as he laid down and adjusted his rifle to point at the grass clearing.

I reached into my bag, took out the 9mm and put it in my waist.

"How was it, working in corrections? I've heard all these wild stories about men raping each other in prison."

"I never worked in a male prison."

"Where did you work?"

"Bention; the female prison a few miles away from here. I worked there for forty years. I had the best time of my life. I met my wife in prison. We had three children, but she passed three years ago." I heard some sadness in his voice. "From the first time I met her in prison, I knew she was innocent; not like all the other Niggers who were claiming they were wrongly convicted."

"There were a lot of Niggers in the prison?"

"That's where they all belong, my friend. And we had fun with them too. We had black pussy any time we wanted. Those who wouldn't fuck us for a cigarette or some clothes, we took those asses anyway."

"What do you mean by you took them?"

My father looked around, like he was afraid someone might overhear our conversation in the woods. "We held them down."

"You mean you raped them?"

"Are you a liberal, Son?"

There was a certain irony in my father addressing me as "Son." "No, but I believe in calling a Nigger a Nigger and a Spic a Spic."

"You're right, Son, and those Niggers were the sweetest. Boy, did they put up a fight." My father laid the gun down and turned around to describe the women. "Those who fought, we treated them the worst. We would punch and kick them like they were dogs; then one of us would get on top and stick it in. We'd take turns until we all got enough of what we wanted." My father's eyes became dreamy as he spoke. "We would pick them out like fruits in the market. There wasn't one black woman who I wanted that I didn't have."

I hoped my father couldn't see the hate in my eyes but I was trembling. This was worse than slavery. "So what happened if they reported you guys?"

"Report us? Are you crazy?! If they reported us, it would be worse for them. A few of them started investigations after they left, but those never amounted to anything. The warden had his share of women too. Those were the good old days." My father smiled. "Oh, to be young again."

"Did you remember a woman by the name of Sonia Watson?" I put my hand in my waistband.

"Who?"

"Sonia Watson, prisoner 225768."

My father looked confused. "Who was she?"

"She was a prisoner in Bention Correctional Facility in 1967."

"That was my second year as an officer. We had a lot of fun that year. Who is she to you?"

"Do you remember her?" I asked, holding the deep blue eyes of my father.

"No. What is this? Are you a cop?" my father asked nervously.

"No, I'm not a cop."

"Reporter?" My father clutched the rifle.

"No, she was the first black queen of New York."

My father lifted the gun to my head. "I knew that you didn't belong here. What do you have to do with that whore?"

My sweaty finger reached around the trigger. My eyes didn't blink. "She was my mother!"

"Oh, she put up one hell of a fight, but she was the best. We saved her for a special night. I think we did her on New Year's Eve. She was the only one who hadn't been touched since she had come into the prison. No; she thought she was too good for us. We tried everything to get her, but she wouldn't let any of us touch her. She thought she was too good for us. So that night we fixed her good."

"No."

"Yes, we did. There was a party that night and your mother had her ene-mies." I could tell the recollection was getting to my father. Saliva drooled from the sides of his mouth. "We knew that she wouldn't go to the party so we went to her cell after the party had started. That night we had smuggled whisky in for the ladies and, while they were having their party, we had ours with your mother. Sit down, Boy. Let me tell you what happened to your mother." Jim motioned with his rifle for me to sit down.

"No."

"I said sit your mother-fucking Nigger ass down." This time, my father put the end of the rifle in the middle of my forehead. "Remember, accidents happen in hunting. If you don't believe me, ask our vice president."

I sat down. "Are you going to kill me?"

"Oh, I stopped killing Niggers a long time ago. There are too many com-plications involved with that, but I'll give you one hell of a good beating. Your mother was a fool and I see the apple hasn't fallen too far from the tree."

"You will suffer for what you did to my mother."

"Maybe, Boy, but not in this lifetime. Life has been very good to me. After I finish beating the hell out of you, I'm going to kill some deer; then I'm going to put out an SOS. Nigger needs help! He's fallen and can't get up." My father was smiling.

Ants had started to crawl onto my skin. "What then?"

"Don't worry about that, Boy. Everyone will hear your story. The same story your mother told thirty-five years ago. Yes, we raped your mother and we beat her until we thought she was dead. But your mother was a strong woman; she didn't die. She held onto life as she was rushed into the hospital. I think she spent two months in that God-awful place. I heard she lost her hearing in one of her ears. We tried to kill her in the hospital but the stupid Nigger we talked into doing the deed got caught while she was choking her. Then we heard that your mother was pregnant and the warden arranged for her parole. I told the other fools who were with me that we should've made sure that she was dead in the cell. I heard she died before she could deliver."

"No, she didn't."

"What!" My father was stunned. He looked at me to see his reflection. The gun started to slip from his hand.

An opportunity presented itself.

"Who…"

I took advantage of the opportunity. Before the gun could fall to the ground I grabbed a hold of it. My father kept looking at me, still in total shock. I put the gun under his chin. His mouth opened to say something but the time for talking had passed. My fingers slipped over my father's and the trigger was pulled. The shot had started the hunting season.

I didn't go back to my hotel. Instead, I called Marge while I walked back from the woods. She picked up the phone on the second ring.

"Hello." She sounded surprised.

"Why do you sound so startled?" I asked. I had a slight headache.

"I didn't expect to hear from you. Aren't you out there hunting?"

"I'm a little embarrassed," I replied.

"What happened?"

"I got lost and called out to my friends but I couldn't find them. What are you doing?"

"Bored; sitting here watching porno movies."

I liked Marge. "I have condoms."

"Come on over. At least I won't waste this beautiful hotel room."

Did I say I liked Marge? I hung up the phone, with my headache getting worse. I sifted through my bag and took out the pack of Viagra pills. I peeled the paper covering off and pushed one pill out. I swallowed the pill and drank some Nestea. I looked at my cell phone. It was going to take me thirty minutes to get to Marge's hotel.

I knocked on the hotel door. She opened it, wearing a black, sheer negligee. Her breasts were so big they looked like they would burst and her thighs were fat with rows of cellulite. I looked her over and smiled.

"Are you ready?" she asked.

"Yeah, my headache is gone" I said.

Marge reached out, grabbed my hand and pulled me into the room. She dropped down on her knees as if to pray but instead she unbuttoned my pants.

My dick sprang out. Marge immediately took it into her mouth.

I felt relaxed knowing that today I had killed a white man and now I was going to fuck a white woman. My father was dead.

CHAPTER 8
13TH DAY

"It's been good to be off for the last month. This is the best company I have ever worked for," Brian said as he opened the door to his apartment.

"I'm hoping to take a year off in thirteen days," I said, following Brian into his apartment. I handed Brian my jacket and he hung it next to his in a small closet by the door.

"Yeah, Man, I'm counting on that myself. Maybe I'll finally be able to move out of this apartment. Rent in Brooklyn is ridiculous. I went apartment hunting with Julie last week and the only decent apartment was going for three thousand and it was a two-bedroom." As was our ritual, Brian went into the refrigerator and pulled out two bottles. He gave me a Heiny.

"What the fuck is that in your hand?" I asked, looking at a beer bottle with brown liquid in it.

"It's a Shandy. You want one?" Brian twisted the cap off.

"A Shandy? Does it have anything in it?" I asked, staring at the bottle.

"Yeah, there's alcohol but it's also sweet."

"You are in love, aren't you?"

Brian looked at me with this big smile on his face. "I told you. Julie's the one for me."

"Any woman who can make a man drink something called Shandy must be the bomb."

"She is." Brian lifted the bottle to cheer and I obliged.

"So, are you thinking marriage?" I asked jokingly.

"Maybe, after we do this thing. I have some stuff I need to take care of first." Brian looked down at the ringing cell phone. "Speak of the devil."

"Right on cue." I left Brian to talk to Julie, whom we were meeting at a cafe in the city. I didn't think my feelings for Julie had changed, but the incident with my father had put it on the back burner.

"We have an hour to kill because Julie won't be leaving her mother's house for another half an hour." Brian sat down with his Shandy in his right hand. "I never knew I would love again."

"Why? What happened to you? A bitch cheated on you?" I asked, taking a seat on the couch opposite him.

Brian turned the TV on.

"Life isn't fair." Brian held his face in his hands.

"Brian, you put a little too much into pussy," I said, without thinking why Brian was so distraught.

"I have a daughter."

"A daughter?!" Brian had never spoken to me about children.

"It's always very hard for me to talk about her."

"Why, is she in Australia or something? Did the bitch take your daughter and run away with her? Because bitches will do that; this girl did that to a friend of mine. She took his son and left New York. He doesn't know where the fuck she is. He has tried tracking her down but he can't find her. These bitches are crazy." I remembered my friend, Leroy, ranting and raving when his child's mother took his son and bounced.

"I know where she is, but I can't go near her. She's in California."

"So, why don't you go and see her?"

Brian got up from his chair, put the empty bottle of Shandy down and went into his room. He returned a short time later carrying an album. Brian sat next to me and opened the album. The first picture in the album was Brian, beaming, holding a half-covered baby in his arms. He didn't have to say it but the look in a man's eyes when he is holding his child is priceless. He pointed to the picture. "That was when she was born. She was the most beautiful baby in the world."

"She sure was." I smiled, realizing that I had said the same exact thing about my son.

"This was when she was one." It was a picture of a baby girl holding on to a crib. There were more pictures of his daughter in all different positions. Brian was in some of them and in others, it was only his daughter. The last close-up picture of his daughter was when she was in front of a birthday cake with the number two in the middle. After that, the pictures were taken from a distance with a high-powered camera.

"What happened after she turned two?" I asked.

"By the time Linda turned two, her mother and I weren't speaking anymore. I had moved out and we could barely stand being in the same room together. Don't ask me what happened between us. I don't know. Whether it was her fault or mine is irrelevant. The shit simply wasn't working. But she would always make me be a part of my daughter's life. She would let me keep my daughter all the time and I thought it was going to go on forever." When Brian stopped and looked up, his eyes were swollen with tears.

I felt sorry for him. "Did something happen to your daughter?"

He shook his head. "No, nothing like that."

"So, your daughter is still alive?" I asked.

"Yes." He continued to stare out into space.

"Why don't you go see her?"

Brian closed the wallet and gripped it tightly in his hands. "My child's mother met someone and he was very insecure."

"That's his problem. Let him go get counseling," I said.

"She said I couldn't see my daughter anymore."

"Okay, bitches say shit all the time. Who gives a fuck?! What the fuck, she's not God!"

Brian shook his head. "God she isn't but she's willing to go places even the devil won't go."

Brian didn't have to say any more because I knew exactly what was coming next.

"That would have destroyed you and everyone around you," I said.

"I would never do anything like that. God knows I would kill anyone that even comes close to my daughter with that. It hurts. It hurts. It hurts. I have never held my daughter in my arms since then." Brian started to cry. The tears were uncontrollable and unstoppable. It shook his body on this Sunday afternoon.

I put my hands around his shoulder to comfort him. "Your daughter is getting older and one day you'll be able to talk to her and tell her the truth."

"But I'm missing so much," he said between sobs. "She'll never forgive me."

"Brian, there's nothing you could've done. When a man is accused of sexual abuse, the accusation is a loss. It doesn't matter who finds you innocent. There will always be questions. People who are willing to put stuff like that out there for their personal gain are sick; it's a sickness that no fire burns hot enough to punish them for. Your daughter will be old enough soon, when the mother cannot pull something like that, and you can go back then. You can go back and take her away from that bitch. I also bet you a million dollars that the man she did that to you for is long gone. Bitches like that can never keep a man."

My phone chimed and it was a text message from Julie. "Brian, it's time to start over. Julie's on her way to the restaurant."

Honeysuckle Café was a new restaurant located in the western end of Brooklyn. It was the only soul food restaurant that served only brunch and dinner in Brooklyn. The parking lot was manned by a uniformed armed guard who directed my car into the half-full parking lot. I pulled up between a blue Jaguar and a white Cadillac Escalade. I turned the engine off, putting an end to a *Strickly the Best* CD that Brian had popped into the sound system.

There were two huge pillars painted in red, yellow and green with an entrance sign between them. The rest of the building was multicolored in red, yellow, green and black.

"This is different," Brian said as we walked toward the pillars.

"The black man is doing his thing. This is no Flatbush. Somebody paid a few dollars to build this," I said, walking up to an attendant dressed in a white shirt and black pants standing at a huge mahogany door.

"Good afternoon, Gentlemen. Party of two?" He held the door for us to enter.

Brian placed a few dollar bills in the man's hand. "Our company is already inside."

"Thank you, Sir," the attendant said as the money disappeared into his pocket.

"You're being generous today," I said to Brian as the attendant eased the door shut.

Brian searched the room for Julie. "In spite of all the ups and downs, it's still a good life."

Anyone who knew anything about restaurants would have quickly concluded that this was an expensive one. There was ample spacing between the tables, instead of them being scrunched together like normal, economical restaurants. The tables were made of high quality wood and the clear table coverings ensured that diners could admire their beauty. I alerted Brian when I spotted Julie waving her napkin. We pointed in her direction and the maitre d' escorted us to where she was seated.

"Two brothers, over six feet tall, physically fit and dressed to impress; you two attract a lot of attention." Julie laughed. "Most of the women, and some of the men too, all had their eyes fixed on you."

"Julie, you're not right," Brian said, kissing her on the lips.

I followed by kissing her on the cheek. "Yeah, Julie, the women checking me out I could deal with, but then you had to spoil it with the men comment," I said, pulling my chair out.

"Get real, guys. We're in 2006. If there's a woman looking at you, I'll bet you anything there's a man doing the same."

Brian shook his head. "Maybe we should change the conversation."

I picked up the menu. "I'm extremely hungry."

"This is my third time eating here. Everything on the menu is good," Julie said.

"Well, I want breakfast. I think number ten has everything I'm looking for." Brian pointed at his menu.

"Honey, do you think you want all that cholesterol? The omelet is made with four eggs," Julie remarked, rubbing Brian on the right knee.

I looked around. "Where's the waitress?"

"I asked her to give us some extra time," Julie replied.

"Julie, I've never seen this side of you. You're a control freak, aren't you? Watch out, Brian."

Julie gave me that *I-don't-believe-you-said-that* look. "Donald!"

To me, she was the most beautiful woman in the restaurant. I engaged her eyes with mine, making an unspoken plea for her affection.

"Guys, I want to make a toast." Brian lifted his glass of water. "Cheers to my friend Donald, for introducing me to the woman that I now consider my soul mate, the very beautiful Julie Walker."

Julie was beaming. I felt like Brutus as we clicked glasses. Judas was in this gathering and his name was Donald. I had known Julie for all those years and my feelings for her had never gone beyond admiration. But now, as I saw her huddled next to Brian, my heart was bleeding. I turned away from the lovely couple to find some kind of distraction. About ten feet away sat a group of young people, presumably college students. By his mannerisms, I assumed the boy was gay; even though he was surrounded by four girls. Cultural boundaries had obviously been crossed in that institute of learning. The boy was Spanish, one of the girls was Asian, another White and the other two were African-American.

"Donald, give the waitress your order. She's way too young for you." Julie had obviously found the object of my attention.

I had always stayed consistent with my choice in women. Nationality and age never mattered to me. I would sleep with a forty- or twenty-year-old woman. The one that I was checking out looked to be no older than twenty-one.

"Order for me," I instructed Julie and got up from the table.

"You trust Julie that much?" Brian asked.

"If she cares for me half as much as she does for you, I'll be okay." I had gotten the attention of the young woman and I was sure she would follow me into the restroom.

Julie gave me a killer look, but I didn't care. I couldn't have her so why should she give a fuck about who I went to bed with. I didn't look at her as I walked toward the restroom. The lounge area was as stylishly designed as the restaurant; there were two big couches and a few lounge chairs. On the wall there was a pay phone for someone who, for some godforsaken reason, had forgotten their cell phone. The plasma located on the left side of the wall was approximately twenty inches in length. The men's room was located to the left of the lounge and the women's on the right. I didn't have to wait long before she appeared. Her walk was pronounced, yet very sexy, and her tight jeans sent praises to youth. I could tell that she was a woman who got what she wanted; even at such a tender age.

"You were waiting for me." She made it more of a statement than a question.

"I was waiting." As always criminal activities were the main topic in local news. I didn't want to watch it but the location of the TV didn't give me an option.

"Any woman at the tables could've followed you into the restroom. You and your friend really made an entrance but I see that he's taken. So, what do you want now that you've gotten my attention?" She sat down on a beige chair and crossed her legs. She might have been young but her upbringing must have had some money input.

Our age difference did not give her the right to ask that question. "Shouldn't I be asking that question? I'm old enough to be your father."

"If you were interested in being my father, we wouldn't be in this room right now. Besides, I already have a father." She was confident. I liked that. "I'm twenty-one, presently a junior at Columbia, and I'm sure you can tell the kind of men I like. You don't have on a wedding ring, which means that you're not married; or you took off the ring because your wedding vows didn't include forsaking all others."

"How much time do you have?" I asked.

"This is my father's restaurant. I'm not fucking you in here."

Even though the thought had crossed my mind, fucking wasn't paramount to me at the moment. "You live on campus?"

"Hell no! My father has an apartment in Manhattan that I'm using while I'm at school. We live in Mills Basin on Livery Drive."

"Who are the friends with you?" I asked, trying to complete her character in my head.

"The boy is Carl and he's gay. He thinks you're hot. The girls are my friends. They're all at Yale, but we went to the same prep school. Don't be so concerned. I don't hang around children. My cell number is 927-678-2344. By the way, my name is Brenda." She stood.

I stowed her number in my phone. "What time is good?"

"That would depend on what you're calling for." She gave me the look that only a twist of the lock on the bathroom door would satisfy.

"Got it," I said and turned my attention to the news. The anchorman stated that they had found some leads in the death of a retired New York City corrections officer in upstate New York.

I didn't hear the door close, but I knew that I was alone in the lounge. I fell down on the couch as my eyes became transfixed on the TV. As always, the anchorman teased viewers with the intro, then went to a commercial. I had avoided the news because I didn't want to see my face as a wanted man on the TV screen. But now they had caught my attention so I sat back and waited through the GEICO commercial and two other car commercials.

"Donald!"

The news correspondent said that the dead man had an argument with one of his business partners before he went out into the woods. Even though the old man was in his early seventies, he was apparently involved in the production of methamphetamine. The newsman promised to keep viewers up-to-date as this story unfolded.

"Donald!"

"Yes?" I lifted my head to see Brian standing by the door.

"Julie thought you were in here fucking the young girl, but when she saw her come back and you still didn't return, she sent me to look for you. What were you watching on TV? You look scared." Brian walked to the TV so he could see what was showing. But the news had already finished and there was a sitcom repeat on.

"You guys get your food already?" I asked.

"Yeah, we're almost halfway finished. Yours must be cold by now." Brian was still looking at the TV.

I got up from the couch. "Well, let's head back."

"So what's up with the little misses?" Brian asked.

"We'll connect on another day," I said opening the door to the lounge.

"She's hot and she does attract attention."

"You're right. She's hot but her attracting all that attention could be because she's also the owner's daughter." I held the door open for Brian.

"People say if you go and look in gold mines, you might find some gold pieces and if you look in sewage tanks, you are apt to find shit." Brian walked through the door.

"Ninety-nine percent of the time you're right, but that one percent of shit you find amongst the gold can stink the entire place up." I closed the door and Brian and I walked back to Julie.

I didn't know what appealed to me about Brenda nor was I sure that I would ever call her. My cell phone address book was filled with numbers of women that I didn't call. It would be virtually impossible to remember where I had met them all. Then, there were those that I did meet and fuck but, with just a name and phone number, my recollection of the time we had spent together often proved difficult. If I didn't call a woman within seven days of meeting her, most likely, I would never call.

Julie and I had been out to brunch a few times and I usually ordered a sandwich or a steak omelet. A deluxe turkey sandwich with Swiss cheese was waiting for me that day.

"I see that you're back to babysitting, Donald," Julie commented as I was about to bite into the sandwich.

I put it back down. "My dear Julie, what's a man supposed to do?"

"Be a man, Donald, and show some kind of control. You're not fifteen anymore," Julie scolded me.

"Why should I?" I asked as I ate some of the French fries.

Julie always chided me for my promiscuous ways. I sometimes wondered if I had a sexual problem, but that would mean I was symptomatic at a very early age. There are a million different ways to handle stress. For me, sex was the only one that worked. I didn't have a drug, gambling or any other dependency so I considered myself lucky.

"One day, Donald, your dick will kill you," Julie said and continued to finish her food.

"As long as it doesn't stab me in the heart. I hate blood."

That ended the conversation. The rest of lunch was all about the food.

"How are you doing, Donald?" Malcolm asked.

I didn't want to be there, much less talk to my father-in-law. "Fine."

"Well, your face doesn't look it," Malcolm said, a glass of champagne in his hand.

We were attending an event in Lauren's parents' clubhouse, located by their private dock. My presence as Lauren's husband had been ordered, not requested. I had walked in with Lauren on my arm like a dutiful husband, which was indeed a painful experience. Malcolm had already introduced me to a few of his business partners who, for a lack of a better word, I found very "creepy."

"I see someone over there that I need to speak with," I said, turning around in a bid to make my exit.

"Donald, have you met Peter and his wife, Kathleen?"

I tried my best to hold on to the apple martini, even though I wanted to ball my hand up into a fist. I had only met Peter once as he was leaving the office. He was a much taller man than I remembered.

He stared at me strangely. "You look familiar."

Malcolm chuckled. "He should, Peter. Donald was one of the main engineers who redesigned your building."

I stretched my hand out to shake Peter's and Kathleen's hands. "Nice to meet both of you."

The smile etched on Kathleen's face did not change; she appeared neither nervous nor uncomfortable. She was so at peace in the arms of her husband. They were indeed a wonderful couple. They reminded me of so many of those pay-per-view movies with the strikingly handsome white man and the extremely beautiful woman getting together after going through some terrible times. They didn't merely get together; they were born to be together.

"I have to pay more attention to the people who come and work in my building," Peter said.

"Don't worry about that, Peter. The security system we've installed would need the CIA and the FBI combined to take it down," Malcolm boasted.

"And we all know that that'll never happen," Peter added.

I laughed at their dry humor. "Sorry, someone is waiting over there for me. It was a pleasure meeting both of you."

I walked over to the bar and started a conversation with a man that I had never seen before. He was an associate of one of Malcolm's business partners. His specialty was foreign imports. After conversing on our employment, he left because he saw someone that he recognized.

I motioned to the bartender. "Let me have some Grey on the rocks."

"Coming right up." He turned to prepare the drink.

"Can I have a Socialite?" my wife, who had walked up to the bar, said to the bartender once he returned with my drink.

"One Socialite coming up," the bartender said.

I glanced at Lauren, then got back to my drink.

"My father said we have to mingle together," Lauren said as the bartender sat her drink in front of her.

"We do?" I emptied the drink in my mouth and motioned for the bartender to refill.

My wife followed suit with her drink.

The bartender looked at both of us and went to refill our glasses. We had two more refills before my wife slid her hand in mine and we headed back out to mingle. It was going to be a long night. It was painful enough driving there with her, but the return trip was destined to be even worse.

Later on that evening, we joined Dora and Malcolm and took a picture as one happy family. Time and faith prevented me from throwing up. My stomach rattled like a pinball machine as the picture was being snapped. My only recourse for the evening was knowing that, soon, I would be able to tell all of them to kiss my black ass.

"Bye, Mom." Lauren waved to Dora before getting into my car.

I nodded my head to Malcolm and Dora and reversed out of the driveway.

"You have to give me another child. My mother insists that we should try for a girl. They're so in love with Emerald," Lauren said, leaning back into the car seat.

If looks could kill, there would have been one dead lesbian in the passenger seat next to me. "What the fuck are you talking about?"

"Donald, why are you acting so surprised?" Lauren asked.

"Because, Motherfucking Bitch, you are crazy. I'm not having any more kids with you. I'd rather go and have my shit surgically removed right this second." I dreaded the thought of such extreme but possibly necessary measures.

"Mom wants us to try for a girl and you know Daddy won't stop until we do it. He said he'll *talk to you* and I know what that means." Lauren looked away. "Donald, I don't hate you like you do me. With all your faults, you're still a good father to Emerald. I don't want to see you get hurt."

The bitch actually seemed genuine when she said that. "Well, Malcolm's going to have to kill me because there's no way in hell I'm gonna touch your ass."

"Donald, do you actually think I'm looking forward to having sex with you? I'd rather swallow a bucket of raw fish gills. Believe me, I'll have to be under the influence, of something, when we do it."

"Don't worry about that, Lauren. We're not going to be doing anything; except I'm going to keep fucking whomever I want while you're eating Annette's pussy. That's all we're gonna be doing. Get that through your cobwebbed head."

The alcohol in my head made me step on the gas much harder than needed. The tires screeched as I took the corners.

"Donald, why don't you get it through your head? You've been bought. My father owns every piece of you. He has your balls in a vise grip and, when he squeezes it, he determines how high you jump. Do you honestly think he's going to take no for an answer? My mother wants a granddaughter and she's going to get a granddaughter. I don't like it, but I've accepted it. Don't act like you're fighting for some kind of rights; you have none. So, take whatever drug you have to and let's make this child."

Every pole that I passed looked like a good way to end it; both of us wrapped around a fucking pole in Brooklyn. Alcohol would've been the main culprit. The only thing stopping me from doing that was Emerald. I lived for him. In thirteen days, I'd prance up to Malcolm and tell him to go fuck himself. Money bought power and only power would set me free.

"You think I'm your father's puppet? My grandmother always told me that every dog has his day and even the biggest dog would one day go down with a whimper. I'm going to repeat myself one last time. I'm not having another child with a lesbian bitch. I don't care if your father's God, it's not happening."

I pulled the car up into the driveway. The lights in the master bedroom immediately came on.

"Well, I tried to make it easy on you," Lauren said, getting out of the car. "But your dumb, motherfucking ass won't listen. I'm not going to let our son see you all fucked up, so we'll be traveling soon."

"You're not taking my son any fucking where!" I shouted. "Now go upstairs and let she-man beat the shit out of you."

For a minute, Lauren looked like she wanted to cry as she turned and walked slowly into the house. She realized that I was right. Annette always started an argument with her whenever we went to a function. An argument that usually ended with Lauren getting her ass whipped.

Emerald was fast asleep and I wasn't in the mood to listen to two bitches that night. I put the car in reverse and backed out of the driveway. I maneuvered through my phone book for Brenda's number and dialed.

"Hello, Brenda," I said as I turned onto the main road.

"What time is it?" she asked.

"One-thirty."

I pictured Brenda wiping her eyes and sitting up on the bed. "What do you want?"

"It's one-thirty," I repeated.

"You're a smart one, aren't you?" She paused. Then she spoke her address slowly and repeated it. "Call me when you're outside the building. I'm going to come down. We can go by the South Street Seaport."

There was a rustling noise in the background as I imagined her getting ready.

I had no desire to drive all night. "But it's closed."

"Exactly," she said; a mischievous edge in her voice.

"I'm not going to have a child with you," I said, losing my reality for a minute.

"What?!" Brenda exclaimed.

"Nothing. I'll be there in forty." I pressed the end button. I needed rest, but first I wanted pussy.

I called Brenda from outside the apartment and waited for her to come down. I was the focus of the doorman's attention as I stood leaning against the Mercedes Benz S500. If I had been a betting man, I'd have predicted that he would've called the police when I pulled up at that time of the morning if I had come there in anything less than a Benz.

Brenda sashayed out of the apartment lobby dressed in a short denim out-fit. While the skirt did nothing to highlight her beautiful ass, the shortness showed off her beautiful long legs. I held the car door and watched her get in. As she sat down, the skirt rose even higher up her thighs. I looked back at the doorman and winked. He scowled at me. I wasn't mad at him. While he was slightly older than me, I'm sure he had constant wet dreams about Brenda. There he was, opening the door for her as she came in and out of the building, smelling whiffs of her perfume and taking in the beauty of her youth and the elegance of her style. In his mind, he might have dreamed about her surrendering herself to him on the carpet in front of the building. Him delving into the lushness of her garden, shredding her skirt and taking her places only his mind could imagine. No, but that was not to be the case. Instead, he had to open the door for her to run into my arms, for me to take her places only his mind could dream of. Yes, and when I brought her back, he would be waiting there to open the door to let her in and wait again for someone like me to take her away again.

"So, what made you decide to call me?" she asked, lifting up her bare feet to lay them on the dashboard.

"Your smile," I said, looking down at her legs.

"You're funny." She giggled. "You're as interested in my smile as our president is interested in democracy in Iraq."

I was trying hard to find a blemish on her beautiful legs but to no avail. Her legs were also lean and firm, the markings of a runner. "How many miles do you run?"

She looked at me. "Very observant. I run four times a week, about five miles every time. Are you concerned?"

"Concerned about what?"

"That you wouldn't be able to keep up," she said with that mischievous smile that nearly made me want to let go of the steering wheel and leap into her arms. Yes, even though this young woman was twenty-one, she had definitely taken Seduction 101 and maybe 202.

"I see that a nice ass is not good enough for you," I said, knowing that she would know exactly what I'm talking about.

"A nice ass. Please, look around. Most black women and Spanish women have nice asses; even white women are coming up in that department. A nice ass might get a guy to fuck you a few times, but if that's all you've got, he ain't gonna come back." Her chemically whitened teeth glistened invitingly. "We sisters can't depend on our pussy to get a man. There are too many out there with that same thing. You're a beautiful man. What does it take for you to make a second call?"

"You're putting me on the spot here, aren't you?" I asked, parking my car across the street from the South Street Seaport. The place was deserted, as expected. I came out the car and waited for Brenda to get out. She got out and crossed to the driver's side. She slipped her hand into the crook of my arm and we started to walk across to the seaport.

"So, are you going to answer me?"

The gentle breeze bathed me with the exquisite scent of her perfume.

"Right now, what I look for in a woman is peace of mind. I don't want to argue and I don't want to fight. Looks are important but, as you said before, it's not everything. I want sexiness, but intelligence also. I want strength but humbleness."

The sound of her shoes hitting the pavement was like a time clock going on and on. We walked past the restaurant and ducked in a corner as we saw a guard passing on the other side. Her breasts rubbed against my chest; rushing even more blood into my already engorged penis. Even though the guard had long been gone, we stood in the corner, our bodies pressed hard against each other. I reached out and slowly removed her jacket. As I let her jacket fall to the ground, I reached down to part her quivering lips with my tongue. As they opened up, I sucked on them ever so gently, feeling her nipples hardening against my chest. She invited my tongue into her mouth and made a sensuous dance with it. I gazed into her eyes and her lust for me was never-ending. I kissed her forehead and traced her face with soft, fluttering kisses, eventually returning to the softness of her mouth. I released her lips momentarily as I unbuttoned her white blouse.

"You're incredible," she whispered, running her hands all over my chest.

When the last button of her blouse was undone, I continued my kisses down her neck and to the life sustenance of her future children. I kissed around her firm breasts, tracing my tongue around each nipple until finally taking one into my mouth.

She moaned and held my head between her hands, running her hands roughly over my head, bringing an even more aroused state to my manhood. I resisted the temptation of lifting her up and impaling her against the wall with my penis. Instead, I continued to outline her body with the flicker of my tongue as I went downward to her womanhood. Her hands twisted and turned my head around; her fingernails gently ran along my neck. Maybe the events of the day or the events of the past few weeks resonated throughout my body, but I needed that woman. I needed to feel, to taste, to absorb and to breathe her into me. I lifted her skirt and hugged her around the butt; enjoying the fragrance of her womanhood as I slowly pulled her black g-string off. The firmness of her ass and thighs made my tongue follow my nostrils to her shaved vagina. I was breaking my rules and I didn't care. My tongue lashed out between the insides of her thighs as she parted her legs to give me total access. My tongue played between them until she screamed.

"Please eat me."

I brought my hands to rest my palms on the folds of her labia. I parted her as her wetness glistened in front of me. It had been years since I had even entertained the thought of putting my tongue on a woman's vagina. Yet, as Brenda's vagina lay before me, I wanted to send my tongue into the depths of her womanhood.

"Please, Donald," she begged.

Once more my tongue lashed out as if being sprung by a spring connecting to her labia and the folds of her vagina. As Brenda squirmed, I feasted on her as if the end of the daylight would be lost to the night forever. Her body started to shake as she took my head and buried it in her vagina. My tongue reached into the origins of her secretion. I had run the New York Marathon and now the liquid of life bathed me. Her body shook while I continued to lick her juices as she bent and squatted obscenely over my face. I was a picture of the birth of man. I continued to lick her, sending my tongue in and out of her until the weakness came back in her legs and once more shook her body. This time, she held onto my head for dear life as her juices saturated my quenchless mouth. When I was about to come up, she started to go down, but I stopped her and kissed her as she hungrily feasted on her own juices. I took out the condom that I had in my pocket and slipped it onto my penis. As I rose, I slipped my hands below her thighs, entering her when I was totally vertical. For the third time, her body started to shake as I continued to unleash my demons. I went hard and fast and, in the space of two minutes, I exploded in her as she barely hung onto my shoulders. It took all my reserved strength to slowly put her back down on her feet. She was spent and slowly slid down to sit on her jacket.

"I have never…" She started to talk, but I rested one of my fingers on her lips as I sat down next to her. She turned and dropped her head in my lap.

"Don't say another word." I wrapped my arms around the beautiful lady. I looked at her and I wanted to tell her that the time wasn't right and what we had experienced was good, maybe even excellent, but tomorrow I would be gone. The war would never stop and the following day I would be somewhere fighting another battle. We had experienced something memorable and if time, the collector of memories, allowed us a moment to reflect, it would bring a smile to both our faces. If by chance, time allowed us to repeat the act, in another setting or under other circumstances, we would be truly blessed.

CHAPTER 10

I stopped my son in his tracks as he headed into the house. "Emerald, please take your bike."

I had removed his bike from the Hummer and placed it on the pavement for him after returning from a morning ride in Prospect Park. Emerald had recently learned to ride without training wheels. He jumped on the bike and quickly pedaled up to the garage. I pressed the remote to lift the garage door.

"Why are you rushing, Emerald?"

"Daddy, I need to use the bathroom," he said before disappearing behind the entry door to the house from the garage.

Emerald had eaten two burgers along with a hot dog and had guzzled down a Snapple apple juice at the park. I told him that he would need to use the bathroom soon, but he didn't believe me. He had already gone once at the park. I hung my bike over Emerald's and walked into the house. When I got inside, he was just coming out of the bathroom. "Daddy, why doesn't Mommy go riding with us?"

"Because she has other things to do, but I'm sure she's taking you someplace this weekend."

"Yep, she's taking me to The Brooklyn Aquarium. She said they got a new whale and it's a white one."

"Wow, that's going to be a lot of fun."

"But, Daddy, does Aunty Annette have to go with us?" he asked, a strained expression on his face.

"I don't know. Does she bother you?" My hatred for that bitch was all consuming, but I attempted to keep my voice calm.

"No, she doesn't but Mommy's always in a rush when Aunty Annette comes with us."

"Well, I'll talk to Mommy and ask her not to bring Aunty Annette. Okay?"

"Okay, Daddy. I love you. I'm going upstairs to get the word game you promised to play with me." He rose from the chair and put the plate and cup in the sink.

I drank half of the water in the bottle. "Did you read your new book?"

"I started but I didn't finish. I can read some of it to you when we finish playing." He started walking up the stairs.

"Okay, Son, I'll be right up."

"Don't be too long," Emerald said at the top of the stairs.

"I won't."

I went up to his room a few minutes later. We played a Scrabble game and then Emerald read me a story. He had a little difficulty pronouncing some of the words but, all in all, he was way ahead of even the first-graders. After that, he fell asleep and I went back to my room to lie down.

The pain in my face was excruciating. I took my right hand and felt around my cheekbone. Blood was oozing from a gash in my face. It took me a few seconds before I was able to open my right eye. At the same time, I pulled myself up from the bed.

"I see that you're up," Malcolm said, his tall figure looming in front of me. As my eyes became adjusted to the room, I saw him wiping the butt of a gun.

"What the fuck do you want?" I asked, a cornered and angry man. I could barely keep my eye open.

"Do you like punishment? Because you knew that this was going to happen." He remained standing in front of me. "I know that life is difficult sometimes, but this one is all we have. And the most important thing is making our loved ones happy. Dora and I have been together for over forty years. There isn't much I wouldn't do for that woman. We both love Emerald and, even though we don't like what has happened to our daughter, we're willing to deal with it." He paused for a minute to catch his breath. "Dora wants a granddaughter. As for me, my grandson is enough."

"So, why don't you leave me alone?" I asked, wiping the blood from my cheek with the white sheet.

Malcolm exhaled loudly. "That's your problem, Donald. You never listen. Dora wants a granddaughter, so Dora gets a granddaughter. You seem to have forgotten who you are. This isn't a debatable issue. You have absolutely no rights here."

"Everyone has rights," I said.

"No, they don't. Everyone thinks they have rights, but they don't. I'm not here to discuss rights. You will impregnate my daughter."

I was barely able to look up because my head was pounding. "Why don't you do it?"

Malcolm moved swiftly for an old man or maybe I had lost too much blood from the cut under my eye. I didn't see the gun coming toward my face. The impact sent me rolling onto the floor. I tried to get up quickly, but I couldn't. I spit the coagulated blood out of my mouth and laid my face down on my left cheek; away from Malcolm.

"I see you enjoy pain," Malcolm said, moving me gently with his shoes.

For the third time in my life, I felt powerless. Here I was, a grown fucking man, being beaten like a child by a man twice my age who wasn't my father. I was in a pitiful state. I lay on the ground, like the bitch I was, knowing that one day my time would come.

"Are you finished? Because I could turn the other cheek," I said.

"I'm finished for today," he replied.

I managed to get my hands underneath me so that I could slowly push myself up. My head was pounding and my right eye was practically swollen shut.

"Donald, I don't like beating you. I haven't had to lay my hands on any-one but you in over twenty years." Malcolm spoke to me as if he was talking to a seven-year-old child. "But, like I said before, I'm willing to do whatever it takes to make my wife happy."

"I have a suggestion. Let me walk away with my son."

Malcolm laughed at me. "Why would I do that?"

I tried my best to look him in the eyes but the pain was overwhelming. "Because, one day, you won't have a choice."

"Donald, you've gone and lost your fucking mind. You're definitely not taking my grandson. The only way Emerald is moving out with you is over my dead body."

I mustered all the strength I could. "Then so be it," I said as I awaited another blow.

"Your balls are growing, Donald, but you're still way out of your league. I have put down men much bigger and stronger than you."

Since shooting my father, I noticed that I had become much stronger. I had killed a man; killing another one wouldn't be that difficult. The only reason I didn't kill my father-in-law that day was because it would have destroyed me. I had to be smarter than that and wait for the right opportunity. We were going to meet again and, the next time, I was going to make sure that I was in a better position to live or die as a man.

"Aren't you going to hit me again?" I asked.

"No, Donald. The next time I hit you, you won't be getting up. I'm going to give you two weeks to get my daughter pregnant. After that, I'll talk to you again. But our conversation will not go as beautifully as this one. This time you could get up off the floor; next time you will lose some limbs. Which one?" he said, smiling. "I'm not going to tell you. But you will lose one limb after another until my daughter is pregnant."

"Might as well start now because your daughter and I will never fuck again," I said. At that point, I didn't care. One thing was certain; there was no way in hell I was going to have another child with Lauren. Emerald was not a mistake; Lauren was. I had been a fool once and that was forgivable. To act foolish again would make me an idiot and I was no fucking idiot.

CHAPTER 11
10TH DAY

The first day of the work week had started like any other. New Yorkers were hustling at the break of dawn. I dropped Emerald off at school before heading into Manhattan where I was meeting a friend for lunch. Even though it was never advisable to drive into Manhattan around midday, I still pulled the car onto the Brooklyn Bridge and headed to the sights and sounds of our trademark city. After deciphering the recent traffic changes, I pulled into a parking lot on 57th Street. The sign on the parking lot advertised the best rate in town; $35 a day. I gave the attendant my keys and started to walk toward the restaurant. I was meeting a lawyer friend who had gone through some serious drama in his life. But, lately, things had been good. The new practice he had opened with an older gentleman was flourishing. He was happily married with a son. His story was enough to fill three books.

Rashaun was a black man and, when I say black, I mean the shiny kind. I spotted him as soon as I walked into the restaurant. He stood out like an elephant amongst chickens.

"What's up, Blacky?" I shook his hand and gave him a bear hug.

"What happened to you?" Rashaun asked, looking at my right eye. "No, let me guess. You had to jump through a window."

"It's a long story," I replied, not wishing to get into it.

"Does it involve pussy?" he inquired, dazzling me with the whiteness of his teeth.

"Yeah, something like that. How are Andria and your son doing?"

"The little man is five now and he thinks he could take me. But I have some moves to show him. Emerald must be big now," Rashaun said as we sat down.

"Yeah, he is and smart as hell," I boasted.

"The boys and I still can't believe that you could have a son so smart," Rashaun said.

"What do you guys mean by that? Emerald takes after his father, the genius." I made an effort not to laugh.

"Okay, Donald, we won't go any further with that one." Rashaun drank some of the water from his glass. "When are you leaving that shitty situation you're in?"

"If I could do it tomorrow, I would, but that's easier said than done."

"Yeah, I feel you. Remember what I had to go through?"

"Yeah, crazy-ass Kim. Have you heard from her since she left New York?" I asked.

Rashaun shook his head. "You had to go there, didn't you?"

"Man, if you don't feel like talking about it, we don't have to."

"Good afternoon, gentlemen. Have you all decided on your order?" The waitress was petite with her hair in a ponytail.

We both picked up the menu and scanned through it the same time.

"Let me have the chicken sandwich," Rashaun said.

"And to drink?" she asked.

"Heineken," Rashaun answered.

My face and my mouth were aching so I ordered pasta with broiled fish; along with a beer. When the waitress had left the table, Rashaun spoke, "Kim called me about a month ago. She left a voice mail saying that she was coming to New York and wanted to talk. She claimed that she had something very important to discuss with me."

The waitress returned with the Heinekens and placed them on our table.

"What's left for you and her to discuss?" I asked.

"I don't really know. I've heard that she's married with a young girl and her career has really taken off in Washington. I would assume that the change of scenery had worked out well for her. I can't think of anything that we would need to discuss."

Rashaun picked up his Heineken. I drank some of my mine as well.

"Rashaun, you never know what women will do. She was crazy about you; I'm sure you knew that. You've gone on with your life and she seems to have done the same."

The waitress reappeared with our food.

"Donald, I don't want to see or hear from that woman. Kim did a lot of damage to me. I'm happily married with a son and another child on the way. My practice is chugging along and, when I wake up in the morning, I don't have to be concerned about what will happen next. Peace of mind is a good thing."

I raised the Heineken to his. "Cheers, my friend, on your upcoming arrival. But, please, I don't want to be another Godparent. We're cool but I'd have to decline."

Rashaun placed the beer down on the table and started in on the food. "I feel the same way. Andria doesn't want to tell anyone about the pregnancy since anything could happen in the first trimester. I assured her that we won't have the same kind of drama we had when Wisdom was born. That part of our life is over."

I looked at Rashaun; he seemed much happier these days. The phone call from Kim obviously had him shook, but he'd soon forget about it and go on with his life.

"That's good, my brother. All that drama is behind you."

"So, what about you, Donald? Can my practice assist you with anything?" Rashaun asked. "And don't worry about paying us; I've got you covered."

Rashaun was a good man. If my situation ever led to standing in front of a judge, I definitely planned to take him up on the offer. But my fight was different. Blood had been drawn and blood would have to be spilled to finish this battle.

"I'm definitely going to keep that in mind. You know your shit. I saw how you got Tyrone off."

Rashaun looked at his phone. "Thanks, Man, but I've got to go. I have to pick up Wisdom."

"Yeah, I know what you mean. I have to pick up Emerald from school a little later myself. Don't worry about the bill; I've got it."

Rashaun rose and I followed suit. We exchanged hugs and he left the restaurant. Kim's call was troubling me. Whenever a bitch calls after a long period of time, claiming to have something important to talk about, it's never anything good. My cell phone rang and I looked at the name, then at the number. Yeah, the saying is true. Bitches are a dime a dozen but ladies are one in a million.

"What's up, Donna?"

This was my second time in Prospect Park for the week. I parked my car on Park Avenue and walked through the entrance on Ocean Avenue. I meandered down to the boat rental club next to the lake. I had taken Emerald riding on one of the paddle boats about two weeks earlier. Donna had instructed me to meet her by the boathouse. I had on a blue and white sweat suit with white Air Jordan running shoes. I spotted Donna in a brown sweat suit, talking to a black man in jeans and a white tee. She waved at me and immediately left the man, who seemed perturbed by her actions. Some women looked good in anything they wore. Donna was one of those women.

"Praise God, you're here," she said as she scampered over to me. "That man was promising me everything. He's a manager at McDonald's, but he's trying to change to Wendy's. He said I could have his paycheck," Donna said as we walked to a small clearing.

"So, did you take him up on his offer?" I asked, a big smile on my face.

"Imagine me fucking with a manager from a fast-food restaurant. I'm glad the brother has a job, but you know my lifestyle. I need a bankroll, not a hundred-dollar bill. I already make four times his salary. What the hell? I'm going to get a discount on a Big Mac? Plus the motherfucker has three kids." She stopped at the clearing and opened her feet until they were shoulder-length apart.

I stood next to her and reached down to touch my toes. "Maybe he's first-rate in bed."

Donna went from her feet being shoulder-length apart to a complete split.

"Dicks are a dime a dozen. That brother isn't even playing on the same field as me. Even if we weren't involved in this venture, I still wouldn't fuck with him."

"You want to dine in five-star restaurants, where the check is never questioned?" I asked as I lifted my hands into the air and stood on my tiptoes.

Donna glared at me like I was asking a stupid question. "Dating him would be like you dating a crackhead with no teeth. A sister can only stoop but so low."

I took my left hand and pushed against that side of my face, then I did the same with the right hand. I turned my head around, hearing a slight crackling sound as I worked my head. "I guess you'll never date your plumber."

"Yeah, I would, if he owned Roto-Rooter. Are you ready?" she asked.

"Let's go," I said.

We joined the rest of the joggers and bicyclists on the trek around Prospect Park.

Donna jogged effortlessly. "I see that you're a runner."

I matched her step for step. "I try to mix it up with cycling."

"I'm bringing someone else on board," she stated nonchalantly.

"Are you asking me or telling me?"

"Both."

"Why do you want to involve someone else?"

"I won't be able to be there so we need someone to give you the signal."

We started up a small hill. "Well, don't you think I should be choosing that someone, if it deals with communication between me and them?"

"I have no problem with that, as long as the person is trustworthy and they're not part of our deal. The person I had in mind would be doing me a favor. I'm also in the position to fuck up his life, if I so choose." She increased her pace as we came down the hill. "I don't care who you get, as long as the person knows absolutely nothing about what's going down and the take. Anything you decide to give him would be coming from your end. My guy wasn't getting anything."

I kept up with her, doing longer strides. "Don't worry about that. I'll have that covered. What's up with Kathleen?"

"She said she saw you and your wife at the party. She said you have a beautiful wife." A visible smirk came on Donna's face.

"I'm sure you know about doing your wifely duties. I was simply playing husband. What's your husband's name anyway?"

Donna stopped and I followed suit. "Are you implying that I don't love my husband?"

"Whether you love him or not is absolutely none of my business."

"Just because I have a little fun on the side doesn't mean that I don't love my husband." Donna turned around to look directly into my eyes. "Well, let me tell you something. I've been with my husband for over ten years and there isn't a man alive that I would trade him for. That man is part of my soul."

I yawned visibly. Whatever love Donna had for her husband was none of my concern. "Are you finished?"

Donna realized that her affirmation of her love for her husband had been wasted on me. "Go to hell, Donald."

"Does that mean that you, Kathleen and I won't be getting together again?" I was trying to piss her off even more. "I thought we had a good time."

"We did, but I've had better," she said, widening her stance.

"Maybe I need to try harder." I brought my heel to the back of my thigh. "They say it's always better the second time around."

Donna reached into her pocket for her keys. "Donald, I'm going to give you a call, *if* I need to talk to you."

I watched Donna disappear behind some trees on her way to the exit. Even though the run wasn't even close to what I was used to, it energized me. The swelling on my face had gone down so that it was barely visible. I wanted to go home and be with Emerald but the thought of dealing with Lauren and Annette on any level did not sit right with me at that moment. I took out my cell phone and called Julie. She didn't answer. I called Brian but his cell phone went straight to voice mail. I scrolled through my address book looking for a number to call. It was filled with female numbers and a few males. I put the phone back into my pocket. I needed a shower and a few hours to relax. I slowly walked back to the car. A slight headache started to play with my nerves. Yes, I was going home. Home was where both my headache and my salvation resided.

CHAPTER 12
9TH DAY

"Donald, you're taking all the risks, yet you have to cut it down the middle," Julie said; a cold harshness in her voice. "Granted, Donna was the one who brought it to you and helped plan the robbery, but do you think that she deserves half?"

"Julie's right, Donald. Donna doesn't deserve half," Brian said.

"How much do you think she deserves, Julie?" I asked, looking at her across the table. She had previously informed me that it made her uncomfortable when I looked at her.

Julie averted her eyes. "To be honest, I don't think she deserves anything."

"And you, Brian?" I asked.

Brian glanced at Julie. "I'd say give her twenty-five percent."

"She'll be mad," I said, "and that could create major problems."

"Do you care?" Julie asked.

I didn't know exactly how to answer. It seemed like Julie was trying to ascertain if I had feelings for Donna. "No, I don't."

"What's the most she could do?" Brian asked.

"Well, for starters, she could land my ass behind bars," I said.

"Without incriminating herself?" Brian asked.

I thought about it, but the answer wasn't forthcoming. "I don't know."

Julie straightened herself up in her chair. "Donald, you said you didn't touch the gloves or the knife she gave you?"

"I don't know why I didn't; I guess my body works faster than my mind sometimes."

"So that means Donna's fingerprints are on the knife and the gloves," Julie added.

I saw where Julie was going. "Dropping the gloves and knife at the scene won't accomplish anything."

Julie shook her head. "No, I'm not telling you to drop the gloves and the knife."

"What then?" I asked.

Julie smiled as if an idea for the Nobel Peace Prize had entered her head. "You can kill two birds with one stone."

"How?" Brian asked as we both stared at Julie.

"Listen to this. The only fingerprints on the knife and gloves are Donna's. Now Kathleen is going to take the knife and stab her husband, then give it back to you. Once she does that, the fingerprints on the knife will belong to Donna and Kathleen. You're supposed to give the gloves and knife back to Kathleen, but you won't do that. The gloves and knife will become your insurance policy against Kathleen in case she becomes righteous and..."

I interrupted Julie. "And I will use the same gloves and knife to blackmail Donna."

Brian reached out and squeezed Julie's hand. "Baby, you're a genius."

"How does that sound to you, Donald?" Julie asked.

"It's fucked up, but I guess we could get away with it," I said.

"I still think that we should give Donna something," Brian said.

"Why?" Julie asked, yanking her hand away from his.

"I don't know; maybe it's simply the right thing to do. In life, what we do to others seems to follow us wherever we go. Anyone care for some more lemonade?" Brian asked, getting up from the table.

Brian had obviously become very comfortable in Julie's house. He went and opened the refrigerator and took out the jug of lemonade.

"I agree with Brian. We should give Donna something," I said as I took the lemonade jug from Brian. "We should give her a million dollars so she could hang out on Flatbush."

"Donald, do you think giving Donna a million dollars would make her any less pissed off? There's a big difference between one and ten and when you start adding all those zeros; it only makes matters worse. I don't know what you're going to do, but I say don't give her anything."

"I think we can discuss that some more another time." Brian sat back at the table. "Now, let's go over my role."

"I don't think Brian should be anywhere close to this," Julie said.

"What?" I looked at Julie like she had lost her fucking mind.

"Imagine the two of you, who work for the same company, both being seen in the neighborhood when someone from that company gets robbed. Donald, you're going to be disguised as a white man. There isn't much disguise for Brian."

Julie had a point, but that point also created a question. "So, should I tell Donna to talk to her man about this?"

"Hell no! I don't trust that woman. Any woman who fucks and sucks is twisted." Julie's vocabulary had changed considerably.

"Damn, Julie, I've never heard you talk like this." I stared at Julie in awe.

Brian smiled. "At first, I thought that you and Julie had gotten together but you just confirmed that you all didn't. Julie has an entirely different vocabulary when she's doing her thing."

"Brian!" Julie shouted. "You're going home tonight."

At that point, I had made my mind up. I was going to fuck Julie. I already had strong feelings for her but seeing that other side of her sent my thoughts into overdrive. "Before we go off on a tangent here, let's get back to the lookout."

"Don't worry about that, Donald; I'll take care of it. I'll arrange to have someone as a lookout and that same person will pick you up after the robbery." There was a lot of confidence in Julie's voice. She had everything worked out.

"So, we agree on giving Donna one million," I said.

"It's your call, Donald. If you say a mil, then it's a mil. You know how Brian and I feel about it," Julie said.

"Whatever you say, Boss," Brian said.

I heard them but I didn't hear them. I wasn't the "boss" in this deal; even though I was the main person carrying it out. Sometimes people try to make you feel that you are more than you are. This was such a case. I rose from the chair. "Thanks for your kind hospitality," I said to Julie.

She snickered. "Donald, get out of my house."

Brian leaned back in the chair. "Later, Donald."

Julie looked at him and signaled for him to get up. "I said you were leaving also."

Brian appeared surprised. "I thought you were joking."

"Do I look like I'm joking?"

Brian started to plead. "But I didn't even drive."

"New York has one of the best public transportation systems and, if you hurry, I'm sure your friend Donald will give you a ride." Julie pointed at me opening the door.

Brian went over to kiss Julie. As he tried to kiss her on the lips, she turned her face so that he could only kiss her cheek.

"Bye."

"I will call you later," Brian said and joined me at the door.

"You are a little freak, aren't you, Julie?" I asked, smiling.

Julie came over and slammed the door in our faces.

When we were on the Belt Parkway heading to Brooklyn, Brian and I spoke for the first time since leaving Julie's house.

"Julie really doesn't want to give Donna any of the money. Do you think that's fair?" I asked Brian.

"Julie's a good woman. She's the best woman I've met since I've been in New York. Is it fair to cut Donna out completely? No, I don't think it is." Brian hesitated before continuing. He looked out the window, as if remembering something specific. "Will she be happy with anything but what you guys agreed upon? I don't think so. Hence the dilemma. If she won't be happy with anything but the full thing, giving her some or a little bit will have the same effect. And, to be honest, everything comes back to you, Donald. Donna doesn't know about Julie and me. You have to ask yourself what you could live with. It's not about Donna's feelings anymore. It's about yours."

I heard Brian loud and clear. Since the incident with my father, I had cared less and less about people and their feelings. The world was full of the plighted and seeing that heaven and hell were not certainties, one's actions became meaningless. The mere fact that I was planning a robbery that would involve hurting another spoke volumes about my moral decline. I had rolled the dice; now I had to deal with the numbers. "I really don't have any feelings for Donna. She was a good piece of ass, but I won't lose sleep over her being angry at me."

Brian glanced over at me. "Then there isn't anything more to discuss about this matter."

The rest of the ride to Brooklyn was spent in silence. Brian was immersed in his own thoughts and I was immersed in mine. I was contemplating how I was going to approach Julie and, even though this last meeting had taken her off the pedestal, she was still my friend. I also knew that I couldn't just fuck Julie and keep it moving. I needed someone else to talk to about that so I dropped Brian off at his apartment and headed over to someone whom I could trust.

It seemed like every time I went over to my grandmother's house, I had to drink a cup of tea. Grandma sat on the couch opposite from mine; the hot cup of tea in her right hand. I placed mine down on a saucer on the center table that was covered in a white tablecloth.

"I always thought that you should've gotten married to Julie. Julie's a good girl. She came by to see me last week," Grandma said. "We had tea and a very good talk."

Julie had taken a liking to my grandmother the first time they had met and she had continued to visit her. My grandmother welcomed her visits and, of course, she got to serve tea.

"Grandma, I'm interested in Julie as more than a friend," I said a bit nervously. The only other woman I had spoken to my grandmother about was Lauren and she had told me not to marry her.

"You finally came to your senses. What about Lauren?" she asked.

"Well, with the exception of Emerald, Lauren and I live totally different lives. I hope she will come to her senses soon so we can go our separate ways." I finally drank some of the tea. "We've been talking about getting a divorce."

"You're not going to leave Emerald with those people, are you?"

"Not if I can help it."

Grandma never said "lesbians" or "gays." She always referred to them as "those people" almost like they were aliens. The other day, she had informed me that "those people" were demonstrating again.

"I'd love to see you with the right woman. You've been through so much. I've tried my best to raise you the way your mother would have wanted. You've done a lot of things I didn't like but, for the most part, you've been the star in my eyes. I don't know how much longer I have on this earth, but I'd like to leave it knowing that you're happy."

"Grandma, you're not going anywhere."

She was making me sad. Besides Emerald, Grandma was my only family. She was an only child so there were no cousins or other relatives.

"Donald, I know you don't want me to go but my time is coming. I've lived a long life and when God says it's over, I'll be gone. You have Emerald and he's your responsibility. If you have to fight for him, you do that. If you have to cry for him, you do that. I know you've been telling him about his grandmother. That's very good. He's going to be great one day." She picked up the teacup again.

Grandma had given me a small album with pictures of my grandfather and my mother. She had told me the stories behind the pictures. I had shown Emerald the pictures of his family and explained each one of them to him the way my grandmother had done to me.

"Emerald and you are all I have," I said to my grandmother.

"For now, my son; only for now. Soon you and Julie will give Emerald a sister to play with and maybe another brother. I hope to be around to see that."

"Grandma, Julie's seeing someone else."

"Then what made you believe that she's interested in you?"

"It's a feeling. I'm not really concerned about whether Julie's interested in me or not. The man she's seeing is a friend of mine; I introduced them."

"Boy, you are confused." Grandma shook her head. "For all the years you've known Julie, you weren't interested in her. Now that she's with someone else, you suddenly want her. Are you jealous?" Grandma asked.

I had thought about that. I had met a few of Julie's previous boyfriends and I was never jealous. In reality, I was hoping she would meet someone and get married and have kids. She was my friend and I wished only the best for her. The feelings and the sensations I was having around Julie were new to me. I had never thought about going there with Julie. "No, Grandma, my soul might be troubled, but I'm not jealous."

"Son, let me tell you a story." Grandma put down her empty cup. "When I was growing up, there were these two sisters. Their mother had an old dress and decided to give it to whichever one wanted it. It was an old and ugly dress so the older sister refused the dress and the younger sister did the same. Now when the mother was about to throw the dress away, the younger sister decided she wanted it, so the mother gave it to her. The younger sister took the dress and made some adjustments."

I sat back in my chair. This was going to be a long one.

My grandmother continued, rolling her eyes at me. "Once the older sister saw the dress, she wanted it. The younger sister refused to give the dress to the older sister because, after all, it was her dress. The younger sister was waiting to wear the dress to her high school prom. But the sisters were a year apart and the older sister's prom came first. Of course, she wore it to the prom. Everyone at the prom saw the dress and the younger sister found out what the older sister had done. When the big sister came home, the younger sister was waiting with a knife. The younger sister took the knife and stabbed the older sister to death. Now the dress that no one wanted went from being a prom dress to a funeral dress. You want to know the moral of the story?"

"Yes, Grandma, I'm waiting," I said.

"The moral of the story is: don't take what you don't want because someone else wants it. You might end up destroying yourself for something you never really wanted in the first place. Leave Julie alone with that man if she is happy with him. You had your chance and you didn't take it."

"Grandma…" I started to say something to her.

"Don't say anything. Your actions will prove your words." She paused. "I'm tired now, so I'm going to sleep."

"Goodnight, Grandma," I said as she kissed me on the forehead.

Grandma was right and I should have listened to her and left Brian and Julie alone, but I couldn't. Julie had ignited a fire within me; somehow it needed to be extinguished. Only Julie had the capability to put out that fire. We were all trying to obtain the same thing: happiness. Happiness for some of us would be a smooth, downhill road. For others, like myself, there would be many bumps and bruises. I had endured my share of bumps and bruises; now I was ready for my reward. Julie was going to be mine.

CHAPTER 13
8TH DAY

I woke up at 5:00 a.m. with a brilliant plan to get out of my hell. At first, I thought by having millions of dollars, I would be able to fight my father-in-law. I would fight him in court, or on the streets; it didn't matter. Money could buy justice or muscle. It was the American way. But my thinking was wrong. My father-in-law would have eaten me alive because my money would be new and new money always attracted attention. The way I was about to obtain the money would make attention a noose around my neck. The more attention I received; the tighter the noose. It wouldn't be long before someone would be dragging my body out of the inlet by Paerdegat Squadron Yacht Club.

I called Malcolm after I dropped Emerald off at school. He seemed elated that I had come to my senses. I asked him to meet me by the running track at Seaview Park within the hour. That would be the first of two meetings. As I drove, I thought about my life and the direction in which it was headed. Was I shaping my destiny or was my destiny shaping me?

I was no longer lost within the comfortable confines of a woman's vagina. I had ventured out as we all do in our lives. I was learning to survive as I went along, with ordinary people like myself being the teachers. There I was about to pull off one of the biggest heists in New York and planning my departure with blood on my hands. Over the past few weeks I had become much stronger. Whether it was a good or bad thing, only time would tell.

I parked my car on Seaview Avenue and walked into the park with my sweats on. The neighborhood had undergone drastic changes since the early nineties, like most of the neighborhoods in Brooklyn. With the infusion of the West Indian homeowners, the Whites had scattered. People have said that if you wanted to find a misplaced stone on a street, ask a West Indian because they are the nosiest fucking people around. Whenever I would kid around with Rashaun about that, he would always laugh. "We're good for terrorism," he would tell me.

As expected, Malcolm was already in the park when I arrived. He didn't want to draw attention to himself, so he had on blue and white sweats. In the five years I had known Malcolm, this was only the second time I had seen him without a business suit on. I was positive he had his licensed gun on him, even though, according to him, I posed no physical threat.

"I always knew that you were a smart boy," Malcolm said as I approached. I walked up to him and looked him directly in the eyes. "You won."

He stepped back a bit before he spoke. "What do you want?"

I looked away from him. "I've thought about it and I'm not the best thing for my son. He'd be much better off if he belonged to you. I have nothing to give him. My lifestyle isn't conducive to being a father. Women are my comfort and I need a lot of them. One day I'm certain a woman will be the main reason for my demise." I spoke, not certain that Malcolm even cared about my issues, but I continued anyway. "To pursue my passion, I need money; lots of money. I only ask two things of you."

"What two things?" he asked.

"I want three million dollars and I want Annette out of the house." I watched his reaction.

He looked away from me, toward the soccer field. "I expected the money but Annette's removal will be difficult."

I wasn't taking "no" for an answer. "Make it happen."

"I've never forgiven my daughter for becoming a lesbian; whether it's nature calling or by her own design. I'm sure she told you about the horrors of growing up, once I found out. I make no apologies for my actions and, if I had to do it again, I'd do the same. My daughter was my lifeline and when it was being taken away from me, I had to fight." He spoke in a hushed tone, as if afraid that the grass would somehow record his conversation. "Think of Emerald, your only son, coming home with a man."

"I'd rather not," I said.

"Then you understand."

"I'm not here to take your confession," I said. It was my way of dealing with my son's future; a future I had no control over. "I don't care what you have to do, but get her out."

"My daughter might do that by herself because Annette is totally against her having another child for you."

I laughed a cold dry laugh. "Malcolm, your daughter's being fed through a straw by Annette. Your daughter can't even raise her voice when Annette's around. And when she finds out that Lauren's pregnant again, who knows what she might do."

"I don't talk to my daughter, but I do understand the effect Annette has on her. I might have to kill her."

I smiled. Now he was talking my language. A thorn that I thought would always be in my side was being removed. I was certain that I would have killed the bitch myself, but it would be better if Malcolm did it. So many things had changed since I had killed my father. I now felt empowered to do whatever I had to do to take care of my problems. Taking a life no longer meant anything to me.

"I believe you can do it much easier than I. I don't think Emerald would be happy with his father in jail."

"You've pushed me ahead of schedule," Malcolm said. "But I've seen my daughter with cuts and bruises and I know they didn't come from you. I agree with you. That isn't a good environment for Emerald."

"Have Dora call your daughter tomorrow and, in seven days, I want my money. I'll give you two weeks to take care of Annette. I'll bring the papers giving you legal guardianship and the right to change Emerald's last name. In return I want you to bring me the three million."

"It seems like you've really thought this thing through," Malcolm said. "What happens if I don't bring the money?"

I confronted him with my eyes. "Then one day you'll have to hire detectives to find Emerald."

"You realize what will happen when I find you."

"*If* you find me. I read recently that they found a child who went missing twenty-five years ago. Are you willing to take that chance? If you are, then we have nothing more to discuss." I turned to walk away.

"Okay, you have a deal."

I swung back around to see him extending his hand to me. "Three million dollars."

"Yes."

Malcolm grasped my hand tightly to see if I would flinch. The time for flinching was over. He held my hand for about a minute, extracting the life blood from it. When he finally let go, I slipped my hand into my pocket; my face expressionless. As I turned to walk away, I knew that the next time Malcolm and I met on those grounds, one of us would not be walking away.

I drove over to Julie's house under the pretense that we would be discussing the robbery. In actuality, I wanted to talk about us. She had told me that Brian wasn't coming over so we could talk. I didn't want to talk; I wanted to take her in my arms and make earth-shattering love with her.

She opened the door wearing fitted jeans and a tight, red shirt with the word "Blackfunk" screen printed in black on the front. "What's up?" she asked, leaving the door open for me to come in.

"I need directions." I walked in and closed the door.

"Where you going?"

Damn, this will make me sound like a child. "To your heart."

"Donald, don't start this." She sounded like I had drained the very life out of her.

I went up behind her. "Don't start what?"

I could hear her heavy breathing as her body fought the temptation to turn around.

"I knew that you would start this. Donald, you don't want me. I've known you for all these years and you've never approached me. Now that I'm in a relationship with your friend, you're bringing this on me." She sat down on the couch.

I remained standing. "Julie, I'll walk away right now if you tell me that you want us to just be friends. I don't know when it happened but, somewhere along the line, I fell in love with you. I touched you and my blood ran ten miles a minute. Can you honestly tell me that our relationship hasn't changed?"

Julie remained silent for what seemed like an eternity. "Donald, you're so damn selfish. How long have I waited to hear you say those words to me? I've seen you through both the sunshine and the rain. I've held my feelings for you under my skin for so long; just waiting. It pained me when you walked down the aisle in this loveless marriage. If you had looked, you would've seen the tears in my eyes, but you were too wrapped up in the glitter."

I was astounded. I knew that Julie liked me but I didn't know the extent of her feelings. Now it was my turn to feel ashamed and stupid. "Julie, I didn't know."

"Of course you didn't know, because you could only see Donald." Julie was crying.

I sat down on the couch and gently eased her into my arms. "Why didn't you say something?"

Julie got up from my chest and turned around to look me directly in the eyes. "You've dated so many beautiful women—doctors, lawyers and models. Donald, how could I compete with those women?"

I kissed her softly on the cheek. "Julie, you don't have to compete with those women. They meant absolutely nothing to me. I've always cared for you but I've always run away from you. You know the life I live. I didn't want you to be destroyed with me. I loved you so much that I didn't want you to get hurt. You have so much to give a man."

Julie rose from the chair and walked away to lean on her bedroom door. "Brian is a good guy."

I remained seated. "I agree; Brian is a good guy."

"I have no doubt that he'll stay with me and be faithful. Brian isn't trying to fuck the world like you." Her voice was stern and penetrating. "To follow my heart and be with you would only lead to failure."

"Do you not want to follow your heart?"

I got up from the couch and walked to her. She took a few steps back into the bedroom. I had seen Julie's bedroom a thousand times but that day it felt like I was seeing it for the first time.

"Donald, there's a big difference between following your heart into eternity, as opposed to following your heart into destruction." She sat down on the bed.

"Julie, I came here to get the directions to your heart. Today, you tell me that I'm already there. You know that I would be lying if I told you that the road I have chosen will be an easy one. Actually, I know it's going to be an extremely difficult one. I'll have to do things that might break me or push me forward. I offer no guarantees and that's the God's honest truth. But today, I'll also tell you another God's honest truth. I love you. In a few days, all hell will break loose and my life will either come to an end or I'll move on with the journey."

I sat down next to her on the bed and took her face in my hands. I pulled her toward me and bent her head ever so slightly as I laid a kiss on her forehead. "It's your decision."

"Donald." She slipped her hand in mine as I got up to leave.

"All I'm asking is that you think about it." I bent to kiss her hand ever so gently. "Tomorrow, I have a terrible job to do."

"Do you want to talk about it?"

I began to make my way toward the door. "Maybe one day."

Julie followed me. "Be careful."

"I will."

As I walked away from the doorway, I turned around to look at her once more. I saw a reflection of myself in her eyes, the reflection of a troubled soul moving toward salvation or an end. It seemed like I had been going back on my word lately and tomorrow wouldn't be any different. Tomorrow, I was going to fuck my wife, something I said I would never do.

CHAPTER 14
7TH DAY

I attempted to fantasize so that my dick would get hard as I sat down in front of the 50-inch Panasonic plasma TV. As was the case with most of the latest black pornos, the women were taking it in all three holes. I was watching *Gang Bang 179* and while I didn't see *Gang Bang 1* through *Gang Bang 178*, I assumed they followed a similar pattern. Some fellas got together and then invited a few women over until dick, pussy, ass and mouth were thrown all over the place. The brothers were huge; the white and black women accommodating. A jealous man would've taken the remote and thrown it at the TV. I wasn't lacking in penis size, yet the brothers on the screen were putting me to shame. With deep concentration and the visual motivation on screen, my penis finally stood up for roll call. This was one time sex was going to be very painful. Lauren and I had exchanged STD test results so, I was somewhat safe to go in without cover.

As I tugged on my penis, my stomach began to rumble. I wanted it to be the shortest time that it had ever taken me to bust a nut. I was hoping to be in Lauren less than thirty seconds before I sent my soldiers hunting. The more excited I became, the more my stomach rumbled.

"Come in!" I shouted.

Lauren came in wearing a pink, see-through negligee. She looked half-decent with her raisin tits and small ass to complement her bony frame. "I thought you would never call me."

"It was difficult," I said as she took her position on the bed.

Her knees were on the bed and her butt was facing the wall as I had instructed her earlier. She pulled her dress over her butt to expose her shaved vagina. A clear transparent liquid glittered between her vagina, with small rivulets running down her thighs.

I continued to jerk faster on my penis as I stood up. I went quickly to her and entered her with the utmost ease. As I went in and out of her, my stomach rumbled even more until I felt it. It took me less than ten strokes before I sensed it coming. I was happy and disgusted at the same time.

"I'm coming!" I shouted.

By opening my mouth, the nausea that had built up in me came out at the same time. My mouth spewed vomit all over Lauren's back and her hair while my little soldiers were in a race to penetrate the cell.

"Oh shit!" She reached around to touch her neck. Her hand became a testament to my meal earlier today.

"I'm sorry," I said, not wishing to make an already ugly matter worse.

"Me too," she said and turned around and spewed her own vomit onto my chest.

I turned away with the hope that her vomit would not splatter over my face. The warm liquid bathed my lower body. I stood there transfixed by the disgusting absurdity of the moment. Lauren got up and ran into my shower. I quickly followed her.

I shook my head as the water cascaded down my skin, brushing against Lauren in the shower stall. "I can't believe this," I said.

"*You* can't believe this!" she replied.

"This is disgusting."

Lauren turned around. "Donald, please get that shit out of my hair." I took my hand and directed the water toward Lauren's long black hair as I tried to remove my vomit. It was the first time I had touched my wife's hair in over three years. I took my brush and brushed the vomit out. The warm water was flowing from her hair down her back. When I was finished, I got out of the shower and handed Lauren one of my towels. I took her negligee that I had previously stepped on as I hurried into the shower and put it in a white plastic bag I had on the vanity. I opened the window to let the combined scents of the sex and vomit out of the window.

"This is a big difference from when we were trying for Emerald," I said, reflecting on our previous lie.

Lauren came out to the bedroom, her small frame wrapped in my big blue towel. Her long black hair was matted against her back. "We're living the American dream."

I slipped black pajama bottoms on. "Or nightmare."

She sat on my bed. "Donald, you need your freedom."

There was compassion and empathy in her voice. It was as if she was caught up in a life that was not her own. "I need a lot of things," I said, wishing I could fly away from there and start life over again with Julie and Emerald.

She rubbed her stomach like the child was already forming. She looked around the room as if seeing it for the first time. "I'm sorry that I deceived you on the day of our marriage."

It was the first time she had apologized for our predicament. "I wasn't innocent," I said, wondering if I would have married her knowing that she was a lesbian.

"What time is it?" she asked in a daze.

"Two-fifteen," I said.

She quickly rose from the bed and removed my towel. She handed it to me and I gave her the vomit-soaked negligee.

"I don't think Annette will take too kindly to meeting me in your room, wrapped up in your towel."

"I really don't give a fuck about Annette's thoughts."

"Well, I do. Annette can be very mean when she wants to. Otherwise, she has a good heart," she said, opening the door.

There was nothing to say. Lauren knew how I felt about her *he-woman*. It was only a matter of time before Malcolm put her into the earth where she belonged.

"Are you going to call the maid?"

Lauren was about to shut the door. "Yeah, she should be here in an hour."

I went to my closet. "My room door will be open, as usual."

"Okay," she said and closed my door.

I took out underwear from my drawer as I thought about what had just transpired. I was hoping not to have to repeat the performance. In seven days, Lauren should know whether she was pregnant or not. I prayed that she was. Although I had no intention of Lauren having my child, I needed for her to be pregnant for my plan to work. As I was walking down the steps to the front door, the front door opened. It was Annette.

"Who the fuck you looking at, Bitch?" Annette spewed, her eyes seemingly wishing a million locusts on my body.

I looked her up and down, then gave her a look of total confusion. "What the fuck are you? Man? Woman? Animal? Reptile?"

She left the door open. "Get the fuck out of my house."

"You know, there is counseling for whatever you have. I'm sure there is help out there for whatever you are repressing. Look on the internet for a doctor or something. You shouldn't go around looking and feeling like that," I said, walking past her. "And I don't think you understand. Just because you're feeding here doesn't mean that the title has changed hands."

"Your wife is mine, Pretty Boy. Don't go forgetting that. I'm gonna go upstairs and have her wash my pussy." Annette's smile was like a grimace and I stood back.

"Don't you mean dick? Oh, I'm sorry; you don't know what a real one feels like. I'll let you touch mine if you promise you won't cry." I needed a little comic relief.

"I'm going to get you, Motherfucker. I promise you; I'm gonna get you and it won't be pretty."

"Promises, promises. Go grow a dick." I slammed the door before she could form a response. As I walked toward the car, I heard the front door open.

"You betta watch your back, Motherfucker!" Annette shouted from the foyer.

I didn't turn around. Instead I got into my car and drove off. I had done what I had to do and now I was doing what I wanted to do. I picked up the phone from the car seat and ignored New York law about driving with a headset as I dialed Julie's number.

"Hello, Donald." Julie never called me Donald on the phone.

"What's up? Are you hanging out with Brian?"

"Yeah, we're about to go eat. You want to come?"

I didn't feel like being a third wheel, especially when I wanted to be the driver. "No, I'm going to take a rain check on that. But you guys have fun."

"Hey, you could call me tonight if you want to talk," she said.

"Yeah, I'll do that."

I ended the call. I wanted nothing more than to talk with Julie. I wanted to be her lover and her friend. Julie was special and even though it had taken me a long time to grow beyond our friendship, the time had come for our worlds to intertwine. I had crazy thoughts about us. After the robbery, we could sail the world; just her, me and Emerald. Wherever she wanted to go, I would take her. When money was no longer an object, the world would become very small. I had always wanted a vacation home in Barbados; now it would go from being a dream to a reality. I had fucked hundreds of women but now I was ready to settle down with the right one. I smiled— that smile you make when you know life's about to take a turn for the better.

I looked at my watch, picked up the phone and dialed Donna's number. I was about to get to point D, but first I had to go through B and C. Donna was B; then later I would deal with C.

"Donald, whatever you do, don't even try to double-cross me. I'm telling you that right now. I will kill both you and your son," she said as we sat in the car.

I reached over and grabbed Donna by the throat. "Don't you ever threaten my son."

She started to make gurgling sounds as I continued to squeeze her neck and pull her up from the seat.

"O…" She was trying to say something to me.

I released her neck. "You can threaten me, my wife or anybody else, but don't you ever threaten my son."

She rubbed her neck as if uncertain that she was still alive. "I'm sorry, but

I wanted to make sure you understand that this is serious business and I will do what I have to do."

Slowly I let myself calm down. Donna had never seen me like that and, from the look on her face, I don't think she wanted to see me like that ever again.

"My son has nothing to do with this. Whatever happens, he's not on the table. I would walk away from a billion dollars if it would hurt my son. But, at the same time, I would kill a hundred men to protect him. In life we make choices; that's what we do as adults. Your kids have nothing to do with this and neither should my son."

I leaned back into the car seat. My hands were shaking.

Donna looked over at me. "You really love that boy of yours."

"Yeah, I do. He's my life. Five years ago, we wouldn't be sitting here. He has changed the way I look at life. It's not all about me anymore." The vibration in my pocket caused me to take out my cell phone. It was Julie.

"It seems like your son isn't the only one who has you preoccupied." Donna had picked up on the change in my facial expression. "Unless that was your mother calling, and we both know it wasn't, only a woman has that kind of effect on a man."

I didn't know I was transparent, but neither was I about to get into my love life with Donna. "Are you sure that Peter will have the money with him on that day?"

"You men and pussy. I know more about Peter than Kathleen does. Peter tells me everything. How do you think I was able to seduce Kathleen?" Donna asked.

"Is that why you wanted to seduce her? Don't get me wrong. Kathleen's attractive, but I don't think you went bush-diving based solely on her looks." In sleeping with Kathleen and Donna I had noticed that Donna wasn't really into women. I was playing that hunch. "I don't think pussy is your thing."

"Unlike man-on-man action, going downtown isn't that big of a deal. In business you do what you have to do to get to the next level. I could live on dick but sometimes, in order to control the game, I have to lick pussy." Donna smiled with an air of confidence. "Peter and Kathleen don't even realize it but I control their household. I always know what either one of them is doing."

"Then why mess with a good thing?" I asked.

"Look at me, Donald. Do you think that this will last? There would come a time when you would walk into the room and I would be standing right next to you and you wouldn't see me. You would be straining your neck to see a woman a mile away. Right now, this is *my* time for men and women to strain their necks to see. I plan to take one hundred percent advantage of it," she said.

I started the car. "Well, if this goes off as planned, we'll both be getting what we want."

"Hey, you got a minute?" Donna asked.

"It depends."

That's the thing about life; it always "depends." I sensed that she was trying to fuck and I wasn't interested at the present time.

"Not that, Donald. Besides, you look like you're in love." She winked at me, still sounding excited. "Seeing that we're in Manhattan, I can take you by my dream store—the boutique I'm planning to buy with my share of the take. You'll love it."

"Give me a minute," I said, getting out of the car.

"Tell her I said hello."

I waved my middle finger from side to side at Donna.

I took out my phone and double-clicked on Julie's number. She asked me what I was doing the following evening. I told her that I would be spending it with her. After she paused to think about it, our date was set. I put the phone away and got back into the car.

Donna gave me an inquiring look. "I must meet that woman who was able to do what I couldn't."

"She's not into games." I started the car once more. "You two will never meet because you're worlds apart."

"Keep believing that, Donald. She has tits and a pussy. She ain't no different than me."

"Where to?" I asked, hoping to get off Julie.

"Take Sixth Avenue and turn on 23rd Street and then back onto Fifth Avenue."

I followed her directions and headed up Fifth Avenue. "You always wanted to open your own store?"

"This is a dream. Imagine me owning my own store on Fifth Avenue. It doesn't get any bigger than that. Did you think I dreamt about being a fucking secretary? Hell no. Who the hell grows up with aspirations of making coffee for their boss? It is true that I took full advantage of this position but, like I said, the pussy can only hold for so long." Donna didn't play with the English language. In no sense of the word was pussy a vagina and dick a penis.

"I guess hard work pays off." I maneuvered around a yellow cab that had stopped in the middle of the street.

"Hard work and some carpet burns." Donna laughed at her own joke. "In this world, it's never about one thing. Some of us might be able to combine hard work and some luck to equal success. Some of us could be in the right place at the right time combined with a certain look and you are tops. Look at you."

"Me?"

"Yeah, you!" she shouted. "Do you think that there are a whole lot of ugly guys pushing thirty-five and living in Mill Basin? You don't think that your brains got you there? Because, if you do, you can let me out right here."

I continued driving, knowing that she was speaking the truth. I didn't have much to offer a woman like Lauren. I was nothing more than a reproductive showcase for her family. There's a saying that states you have to know who you are to get where you are going. I knew who I was and I was about to use it to get where I was going. Donna had said that Julie wasn't much different from her, but I also realized that I wasn't any different from her. I turned down Fifth Avenue.

"This is it. Right here." The excitement in her voice was beginning to make her voice quiver.

I pulled the car over and parked. We got out. I didn't bother putting any quarters in the meter. Donna stood outside the boarded-up two-story building. "So, this is where the new Donna Karan starts?"

"Yep, I'm going to call it Rochelle's, where the fancy people go to shop. We won't be talking about ten-dollar dresses."

"Don't knock the ten-dollar dresses. With the right body, a ten-dollar dress could make a woman look like a million bucks."

I recalled some women from my past. They didn't have the money to buy the expensive clothes, but whatever they wore made them look like they had stepped out of a fashion magazine. One such woman was Carol. Carol was a student attending Columbia on a full scholarship. She lived in the Glenwood projects but you could never tell that Carol was poor by the way she carried herself. She never wore any ghetto-looking clothes that showed too much of the wrong things. She wore clothes that accentuated her positives. Her long skirts encased and molded her long, gorgeous legs. Her mid-cut blouses never fell below her waist; making her ample breasts a feast for the human eye. Her heels were never more than two inches above the ground and her effortless, sexy walk left men longing for a turn.

"I know what you mean. Believe me, I've seen some five-hundred-dollar dresses that I would throw in the garbage before I gave them away. But, I won't be selling anything inexpensive. My store has to be a name-calling store. When women mention that they're going to my store, I want people to know that a Rochelle bag means that the person purchased something expensive. It's like a Bloomingdale's bag, which is a far cry from Conway. I want people to walk around with the bag just because the store is expensive." Donna tapped on the glass window.

"Yeah, I know what you mean. A lot of women put Conway stuff in Macy's bags," I said, laughing.

"You got it; image is everything. There's a black middle-class that has a lot of money to spend while they try to keep up with the Joneses. I plan to help them spend that money." Donna opened the car door. "In the process, I plan on opening hundreds of Rochelle's all over America. Some people merely need a start. What are your plans for the money?"

I was at my worst. Donna had a lot of dreams that would never materialize because she would never get the ten million dollars. Unlike me, she had the world waiting for her respect. The money was going to change her whole life. To be honest, once I came to the conclusion that I would have to kill Malcolm to get my son away, the money wasn't important. I would maybe take Julie on some wondrous trips and put some money away for Emerald. Beyond that, I had no dreams. I didn't have a restaurant that I wanted to open or some plan for a money-making business. As long as my son was taken care of, I was good.

"I'm planning to use mine to get out of hell." I didn't feel like going into details with Donna. "You want me to drop you home?"

"Yeah, maybe you can come in and meet my family," she said. "I already told my husband about you."

"No, I'll take a rain check." I drove down the West Side Highway toward the Brooklyn Bridge. Donna was a true player; she knew introducing her husband to me would take away suspicion. After all, you wouldn't bring the man you're fucking on the side home to meet your husband. This was something a woman could do and get away with but, if a man did that, the woman on the side might flip.

The ride was smooth as we went through Manhattan, then turned onto Chambers Street before taking the ramp by One Police Plaza onto the Brooklyn Bridge. Tomorrow was going to be another day. I had happy plans for the next day. If there was ever such a thing as a soul mate, I had indeed found mine. My only solace in a cruel world was that at the end of it all, Julie awaited. My cell phone vibrated again and I picked it up and looked at the number. It was Brenda. Brenda had a lot going for her, but someone else was occupying my thoughts. I put the phone back into my pocket amid a questioning look from Donna. I didn't want anyone else but Julie.

CHAPTER 15
6TH DAY

I jumped out of the bed as if an explosion had rocked my head. I looked over at the BOSE CD clock on the nightstand. It was 4:00 a.m. I picked up the cordless phone and dialed Julie's number.

"Donald, what happened?" She sounded groggy.

"I'm coming over now," I said and hung up the phone. I went over to the closet and grabbed a pair of jeans. The house was deadly silent as I made my way down the stairs. I turned the alarm off before I opened the door, then turned it back on after I had opened it. I jumped into the S5 and slowly started to back out of the driveway. I saw the upstairs master bedroom light come on and noticed a figure at the window. I pressed the remote button to close the gate. I drove through the streets of Mill Basin, mindful that only the restless souls would be on the road at that time of the night. I hadn't bothered to ask Julie if Brian was with her. I looked over at my cell phone to make sure that it was on. I'm sure if she needed to talk to me, she would have called.

As I pushed the Benz on the Belt Parkway, I contemplated on what had gotten me on the highway. I had thought about Julie before I went to bed and had spent about an hour thinking about us having dinner that evening. But then I woke up and the need to be with her became overwhelming. I didn't want her. I needed to be with her. I had never experienced that feeling before. Yes, on occasions I had awakened wanting to fuck and I had made booty calls that resulted in me getting some. And sometimes, if nothing was available, I would put on an X-rated movie and jerk the fuck off. But this was different. I didn't just want pussy or a blow job. No, I needed Julie right then. I was lost in the desert and Julie was my water. I had lost both my kidneys and Julie had the only one that would be a match. I didn't know when it had happened, but Julie had gotten into my head.

I pulled into her driveway and parked my car behind hers. I looked around to see if any other souls were in my predicament but saw none. There was a car waiting at a stoplight down the block. There were no other signs of human life on the streets of Queens. I walked up to the door. Before I could ring the bell, the door opened and there she was.

Julie was standing in the middle of the doorway in a black, see-through, opened silk robe. The robe barely hung onto her shoulders. I had been with hundreds of women, but no one, and I mean no one, could even come close to Julie. For the first time in my life, I was in total awe of a beautiful woman. I gazed into her eyes and saw a lust that would devour me. I flew into her arms with the fire of the afterburn and as my tongue reached into her mouth, bringing us to a place where dreams were made and lives were lost, I welcomed the loss of my life. She responded by taking my tongue and pulling it into her mouth like it contained the cure for a hundred diseases. I took my foot and kicked the door shut as I relished our passion. The softness of her breasts against my chest, the warmth of her vagina against my leg, was sending my head into orbit. I stepped back from her to open my shirt, but my response was a little too late. Julie grabbed my shirt and ripped it open as I unzipped my pants and dropped them to the floor. She pulled me back into her as I stepped out of my pants. I kissed her on her face, her cheeks, her nose and her eyes.

"I love you; I love you," I said as I kissed down to her breasts. Going from left to right, I sucked them as if they were the juice of life.

"Donald, Donald," she whispered between bites on my earlobe, driving me to a state of frenzy. As I brought my face back up to hers, I went back to greet her tongue with mine. I spread her legs with my arm as she jumped up onto my waist, her secretions warm against my stomach. I went down on one knee, then another, taking her with me to the middle of the living room floor. I quickly pushed my feet out, one after another, as I brought Julie down onto my manhood.

Inch-by-inch she allowed me into her. It was God's wish, the devil's party and our passion. There was no past, no future, just the present and everyone wanted a piece of it. I had never needed to be inside a woman like I needed to then.

"I love you, Donald," she said, as a tear fell from her eye onto my shoulder.

"I do, too, with all my heart," I said as she started to ride me, pulling me deeper into her with every movement. I reached over and brought her face to mine as, once more, I wanted every liquid in our bodies mixing at the same time. I had thrown caution to the wind. If, for some reason, Julie was harboring the deadly sexual diseases of our time, I had given them access to my body. I wanted her and everything that she had. As she continued to use her passion, her body and her spirit, I felt the tremors in her body. Her tremors were soon joined by a weakness in the evolution of man. She had reached out on passion hill to me and together her body shook and my thrust came up in uncontrollable passion. This time it was her who locked my mouth with hers and man and woman were back to their essence. She went into uncontrollable convulsions, taking me and my gift of life far up inside of her. We both fell to the side, my penis still inside of her; our bodies locked together. I stared into her eyes and saw what the angels sang about; what men and women had killed for over the years. I saw a union of two souls.

There were no words to be spoken as we lay locked in each other's arms. Her eyes told me everything that I wanted to hear. Her eyes fluttered, then closed, and I soon joined her in a land where two people who found each other stayed together forever.

"I guess you really like the food here," Brian said as he took a seat opposite me. "Or maybe just the owners."

I had told Brian about my encounter with Brenda, whom I was meeting for dinner. He had called me a little after 2:00 p.m., after I had left Julie's. I agreed to see him before Brenda arrived.

"You want something to drink?"

"Yeah, something very strong, like a Black Man's Heart Attack." Brian drummed his fingers on the table and looked around the room. "Julie has done a complete three-sixty on me."

The waitress had seen Brian take a seat at my table so when I lifted my hand, she came right over. "Let me get a Black Man's Heart Attack."

"Do you want double the Hennessy for five dollars more?" she asked.

I looked over at Brian, who hadn't even noticed the curves on the waitress. "Yeah, I think he needs it."

"I agree," she said with a sexy smile that made you want to holler out her name.

"I don't know what happened with Julie. We were doing so well. Now she doesn't even want me to touch her. Do you think she's seeing someone else? I know she isn't like that but something's going on with her." Brian looked to me for answers.

I drank some more of my Hurricane. "I don't know what's going on with Julie. I know she's preoccupied with the planning of the robbery, but that's about it."

"But, Donald, that shit ain't right. You can't go from being all over me to not even wanting to be near me." He seemed extremely frustrated. "You've got to talk to her for me. You guys go way back. She'll tell you what's going on."

I was the last one to talk to Julie. Even though I felt sorry for Brian, I was glad that Julie wasn't sleeping with him anymore. "Do you think Julie will open up to me, knowing that you and I are friends?"

The waitress put Brian's drink in front of him and he took a long gulp. "Yeah, you're right. She won't tell you anything. She knows you're my boy and you would tell me about it."

"What you need is a woman to get your mind off of Julie; a little thing on the side. Don't let a woman stress you. Did you see the waitress?" I asked.

Brian looked at me like I had cursed his mother. "Donald, I don't want anyone else. I want Julie. I've had my share of waitresses. A phat ass don't mean shit to me. There comes a time when a woman flips you over. Julie's done just that to me and I'm not giving up that easily."

"Take my advice, Brian, don't fight for a woman's feelings. It'll only fuck you up," I said.

"That's easy for you to say. You've never loved a woman in your entire life," he stated angrily. "I can't live like you, Donald. I need more."

"You obviously didn't learn from the past. They say whoever doesn't learn from the past will be punished by the future. In less than a week, you'll have some serious cash that you can use to see your daughter. I suggest you think about that instead of the emotions of a woman."

I looked at the time. Brenda should have been there at any moment. Even though it was her father's restaurant, I told her I would pay for dinner. I asked her what her parents thought about her dating older men. She said they were cool with it, because it was better than her bringing a thug home.

Brian put the glass to his mouth and swallowed the rest of his drink. "Donald, I'm sorry if I was a bit harsh, but Julie is fucking with my head. I don't know what to think. Do me a favor and keep your ears open for me. I want to know if there's someone else in the picture. Here's your young thing." He stood. "She is fine."

I reached out to shake his hand and sat down, my back to an approaching Brenda. She had called me a few times before. I returned her call and agreed to meet with her. When she walked over to the table, I stood to acknowledge her presence.

"You're looking good," I said. She had on form-fitting jeans and a white shirt. Her shiny black hair was combed out so that it dropped down close to her shoulders. She had on some unnecessary makeup because you could tell her skin was spotless below.

She sat down. "Not enough for you to return my phone calls."

I deserved that so I didn't reply along the same line. "What have you been up to?"

"Staying away from the South Street Seaport." She looked me directly in the eyes. "Because good memories are hard to forget."

"Okay, I admit I deserve that, but can we get past it?" I asked.

"If you promise to go with me to Puerto Rico next week, we can." She again looked to me for answers.

"How much time do I have to decide?"

"Not much. I have my ticket. I could buy yours tonight," she said.

The waitress returned with her pad in hand. She looked surprised when she saw Brenda. "Good evening, Miss Jackson, can I help you with something this evening?"

"Donald, are you ready to order?" Brenda asked.

I looked through the menu and ordered the house salmon special. Brenda ordered the steamed lobster. The waitress took our menus and left.

"How often do you eat here?" I asked Brenda.

"Not very often. I like cooking and, if I don't cook, I order something in Manhattan. Sometimes I don't feel like coming over the bridge. When you met me the last time, it was because my friends wanted to come and eat here. I think they were more interested in the free meal. Now let's not change the conversation. Are we going to forget about Puerto Rico?"

"There seems to be an ultimatum in there somewhere," I said.

"Well, you haven't called me and, even though we had a great time at the Seaport, you seem distant. Now I could wait and hope to see you again sometime or you can tell me to fuck off. I'm a big girl. I can take it. I thought what we had was special and I hope you thought the same, but only you can answer that. I'm never the pursuer in a relationship, yet I feel compelled to be with you. There, you have it; we are either going or we can thank God for the memories." Brenda looked at me for a reply.

"Brenda, you are a beautiful woman, but..."

"Donald, fuck that shit." Brenda got up. "I don't need you."

She slammed the napkin down on the table and walked out.

I remained seated. A few minutes went by before the waitress returned to my table.

"Do you still want your order?" she asked.

"Yeah, but let me have it to go," I said.

"I'm getting off in an hour if you want some company," she said, that "holler" smile on her face.

"No, I'll take a rain check on that. But I could do with another Hurricane."

"Well, this one is on me and my offer still stands."

I reached out and grabbed her hand. "You don't want any part of this."

She squeezed my hand. "Yeah, I do. I'm sure you live a very interesting life. Look at you; not too many men are able to walk away from a woman as beautiful as Brenda. She has had men breaking down in tears over her, but you didn't hear that from me." She slipped her hand out of mine.

"Brenda is special," I said.

"But so are you. I've got to go before I get fired. I'll be back with your drink."

"Thanks," I said as she walked away.

"**D**amn." I got out of the bed with a slight headache. The persistent ringing of the doorbell was driving me nuts. I knew the reptile was somewhere in the house and I wondered why she hadn't gone to the fucking door. She hadn't worked a day since she had moved into this house. I went into the bathroom, washed my face and brushed my teeth. There it went again. I looked at the clock radio as I walked out of the room. It was 10:00 a.m. Maybe the reptile had gone out. I snatched a shirt out of the drawer and put on the same jeans I had worn the day before. I was about to open the door when I heard her voice.

"Donald, the cops are downstairs waiting for you," Annette said.

"The cops?" I asked, startled.

"Yeah, the cops," she replied. "Maybe they'll put your ass away for the rest of your sorry life."

I swear I'm going to kill that bitch. Fuck Oprah and what she said about not calling women bitches. That reptile outside is a bitch.

I nervously buttoned up my pants and headed downstairs. "Where are they?" I shouted.

"Downstairs having donuts. Where the fuck you think they're gonna be?" Annette answered for everyone in the house to hear.

I walked downstairs and saw two white men in the informal dining room. They were standing up, their hats in their hands. "Good morning, Officers," I said, extending my hand.

The older man, maybe in his late fifties, shook my hand. "I'm Officer Summers from Ketonya County and this is Officer Sindrel."

I reached out and shook Officer Sindrel's hand. I was hoping that they wouldn't notice that I was nervous. I offered the officers a seat on the sofa.

"Thank you, but this shouldn't take too long." Officer Summers took out a small notepad. "You own a 2005 Hummer, New York license plate DRC7689."

"Yes, it's one of the family cars," I said, sitting down.

"Family cars? Does that mean other people in the household drive it?" he asked.

"Yes, my wife drives it on occasion," I answered.

"Can you recall who drove it approximately three weeks ago to upstate New York?" Officer Summers looked over at me.

"Exactly what day was that?" I asked.

"That would be a Saturday." Sindrel spoke for the first time. "Yeah, that was me. I went to visit a buddy in Buffalo. He bought a house on Rounds Avenue. It's a beautiful place but a little too slow for me." I made a mental note to call my friend, Hill, who had recently moved to Buffalo.

"Did you stop at a restaurant while you were driving out there?" It was Summers asking the question again.

"Yes, I did, and that place was a madhouse. I think they had some kind of hunting meeting going on." I looked at Summers. "Officers, can you tell me what this is about?"

"Well, an older man got killed with his own gun and we're trying to understand what exactly happened," he said.

"I'm sorry to hear about that," I said, hoping that I had the most sympathetic look on my face.

"Well, this is the first time we've ever had something like this happen in Ketonya County in twenty years, so we want to make sure that it was an accident. Hunting is one of our biggest tourist attractions. We definitely don't want to ruin it," Summers said.

"The place sure seemed like a happy place when I was there. People were so friendly. Maybe one day, I'll try that hunting thing," I said.

"We'd be glad to have you. Before we go, did you happen to see any suspicious characters hanging around?" Summers asked.

"I don't exactly know what you mean by suspicious. There were so many guns there but everyone seemed intent on killing the big one." I rose from the chair.

"Yeah, we're having a great hunting season. I think it's one of the best in years," Summers said. "Well, thanks for your time. I hope we didn't cause you any inconvenience."

"I'm sorry, Officers. I didn't even offer you guys something to drink," I said.

"No thanks; we just stopped at Wendy's and had a big meal. Take care of yourself and we hope to see you in our woods next year," Summers said as he opened the door.

"Good day," Sindrel said as he followed Summers out the door.

I closed the door and listened to their car driving off. I went into the refrigerator and poured myself a glass of orange juice.

I walked back up the stairs, passing Annette as she was walking down.

"Freeloader. I thought they'd taken you away," Annette said, her mouth in the same position it had been in before; unnatural.

"Why don't you get an operation?" I asked.

She glared at me. "An operation?!"

"Yeah, your mouth is perverted. Oh I'm sorry maybe that's asking too much because your whole body is perverted."

"You should lock your door at night," she said.

"Why? You might try to rape me? I know your type. You all just want some good dick to straighten you out." I laughed.

"Motherfucker, your time is coming."

I entered my room and shut my door, then laid back down on the bed, still shaking from speaking with the officers. That was a close call. It was obvious that they didn't have me on camera because they were only trying to establish presence. I surmised that they had someone taking down license plates of all the vehicles that were in the parking lot that day. I took my clothes off and went into the bathroom to take a shower. While in the bathroom, I reminisced about the shower I had taken with Julie. It was one of the longest, most exhilarating baths I had taken. I had attacked each crevice of her body and she had done the same to me. We had soaped and cleaned each other from head to foot. By the time we were finished, we were barely able to walk to the bed. I remembered her collapsing over me and the two of us falling asleep again, totally exhausted. If that was what love felt like, I realized I had short-changed myself for more than 35 years. The memories of Julie had gotten my dick hard. I toweled off as I walked out of the shower. There was a loud knock on the door.

"Donald, Daddy is on the phone." Lauren announced it like I had won the lottery.

My penis immediately became flaccid. I went over to my nightstand and picked up the phone. I hung it back up after I had made arrangements to meet Malcolm at his house.

The full-time maid guided me to Malcolm's study. I dismissed her before she had an opportunity to knock on the door and opened it without knocking. Malcolm looked surprised; sitting in his chair in a light gray suit with a polka dot tie.

"I'm sorry, Donald, I didn't hear you knock," he said.

I pulled out a chair from the table and sat down. "I didn't."

"That was very presumptuous of you." Malcolm looked at me like he wanted to spank me.

"Malcolm, please, the maid called you when she saw me waiting outside, so let's not waste any time. You called me and I'm here. Now, what can I do for you?" I retained full eye contact with him as I spoke. I was way past being afraid of him.

"I don't know what has come over you, Boy, but I think you're treading on very thin ice here," he said.

"Well, let the ice break. If it does, I'm either gonna be cold or freeze to death. Now are we gonna get on with it?" I leaned back in the chair. "I have a lot planned for today so I can't stay long."

Malcolm gave me this smart smile that looked like he was waiting to get my balls over some hot coals. "Dora informed me that you've kept up with your part of our deal."

"I did what I had to do." There was a certain amount of disdain in my voice. "I see that Annette is still alive."

"The time isn't right," Malcolm said. "I promise you, I'll take care of Annette within the week."

I got up to go. "I'm leaving."

"Would you like a drink before you leave? I thought maybe we could at least be cordial." Malcolm rose from his chair.

It was amazing; Malcolm was finally giving me some respect. Whether he liked my attitude or not I wasn't sure, but the respect was present in his voice. "No, thank you," I said and walked out of his study.

"Officers from upstate came to my house this morning," I said to Julie.

Julie opened her mouth as if the world had exploded. "Are you a suspect?"

I had told Julie the complete story of what had happened between me and my father. "No, I don't think so. I think they were merely checking license plates."

Julie still looked worried. "They didn't need to visit you for that."

"I think they needed to put a face to the vehicle," I said, nonchalantly.

Julie stared at me. "You don't seem very concerned."

"I'm not. Their questions were more about doing their job than actually following leads. Of course, if I had run when they walked in, that would be an entirely different story. But, with the exception of Annette being her bitchy self, everything went good," I said.

"You're definitely not afraid?"

"I don't think there's anything to fear. I'm more concerned about the robbery. Do you definitely have someone to pick me up?"

"I'll be there," she said.

"You!" I jumped out of my chair.

"Yes, me; I only trust myself. Anyone else, I would have to tell them too much," she said. "Don't worry; I'll definitely be careful."

"Are you sure you want to do that?" I asked, not wanting to endanger her.

She ran her hands over my shoulders. "Stop worrying about me, Donald. I can take care of myself."

"Julie, I don't know what I'd do if something happened to you." I felt really messed up for involving her.

"Donald, the same way you trust me, I also trust you. I have no intention of letting anyone pick you up. We're in this together. The only reason I didn't tell you before was because I knew that Brian would never let me do it." Julie kissed me on the lips.

I shook my head. This was becoming complicated. "I don't know, Julie."

"Donald, please stop trying to protect me. I'll be fine." Julie put her hands around my neck.

While I agreed that Julie should be the one to pick me up after the robbery, I was afraid that she might get caught up if there were any complications. I knew that I was letting my feelings control my judgment but I didn't care. I had found something special with Julie and I didn't want to lose it just yet.

"Alright, but promise me that if you see or hear anything crazy you'll leave."

"Crazy like what?"

"I don't know. If you hear gunshots or spot me running with someone chasing me."

She looked at me as if I had lost my mind. "I'm supposed to leave you to get shot and run home? Or leave you bleeding on the street while I run home and watch TV or something? Let's change this topic because I won't be doing any of those things." She yanked her hands away from me. "Brian told me that he left you with Brenda last night. Did you have fun?"

"Are you jealous?" I asked, pulling her by the hand.

"No, but I know you."

"Well, I've changed. I realize that's hard to believe but I have. I turned down a trip to Puerto Rico with Brenda."

"You're telling me that you didn't sleep with Brenda?" Julie asked.

"I'm not saying that. I'm saying that since I've been intimate with you, I haven't slept with anyone else. Again, I know it's hard to believe, but it's the truth." I hugged her around the waist. "For the first time in my life, only one woman will do and that woman is you."

Julie turned around to look me directly in the eyes. "You are serious."

"I swear on my dead mother's grave," I said.

"Donald, what took us so long? I haven't been able to even touch Brian since we made love. All I do is think about you, morning, noon and night." She ran her hands over my eyebrows.

"So when are you going to tell Brian?" I asked.

"There goes the hard part. Brian is such a nice guy, but I want you. I've always wanted you. It took you a long time to realize that but at least you did. And with all of that, I'm not too sure about you," she said.

"What do you mean by that?"

"Donald, you don't even know if you can be faithful and I need that. It's great that you can walk away from women right now, but what happens a year or two from now? What happens when the woman that you can't get out of your mind comes along? Are you going to stay true to your commitment to me?" Julie's face had become very serious.

"You're right, Julie. I don't know what will happen a year or two from now. I don't even know what will happen tomorrow. Today is all I have and I'm telling you that you're all I want."

Julie was right. I couldn't give any guarantees. I wanted her today, but tomorrow I might want Brenda or Donna. In an ever-changing world that was full of emotion and conflict, could anyone give a 100% guarantee? What happened when the sex became boring and routine? What happened when the arguments at home hastened your exit to work? Time is all lovers have, but time also changes a person.

"At least with Brian I know he'll be there," she said.

"You're right about that. Brian is much more stable than me. I'm not even going to try to convince you that I'm the right one and that we'll ride off into the sunset together." I disengaged myself from Julie and moved toward the door.

"You are leaving?" she asked.

"Yes, I am. I'm going to give you time to make your decision. And, to be honest, I'll love you no matter what decision you make. It's up to you whether we live a life together or apart. It won't change my love for you. You've already secured a place in my heart." I turned around and kissed her on the lips. "In four days, I'll be free, and with freedom comes choices. You can make yours then." I opened her door.

"Donald," she said.

I stood at the door with my back to her. "Julie, let's leave it at that."

"Can we talk tomorrow?" she asked.

"No," I said. "Tomorrow I'm spending time with Emerald and my grand-mother."

"Does she know about us?"

I started walking toward the car. "Sort of."

"What does that mean?"

I opened the car door. "Isn't that how our relationship is right now? Sort of?"

"Bye, Donald." She closed the door as I got into the car.

"Emerald, Grandma and I have to talk. You can go in the living room and watch your show. Please wash your hands and mouth before you sit down," I said to my son.

"Okay," Emerald said as he got up from the table.

Grandma gave Emerald a half-filled jar of cookies. "Here's a jar of your favorite cookies. You can enjoy them while you watch television."

"Thanks, Grandma," Emerald said as he left the room with the cookies.

"Mama, you know you spoil Emerald," I said. "He's going to eat all the cookies."

"I have one grandson and you used to do the same thing. I used to come home and a full jar of cookies would have only one left in it. And nobody ever saw you take one. They just disappeared in your stomach." Grandma retook her seat at the table.

"Mama, can we go to a restaurant the next time so that you don't have to cook?" I asked, even though I already knew the answer.

"Boy, I tell you every time that I don't have a problem cooking. Your grandma might have gone to a restaurant about five times in her life. Your grandfather always used to say why pay for something you could make better yourself? What restaurants you know that make better food than me?"

It was a winless fight so I changed the conversation. "You went to Doctor Charles yesterday. Is everything all right?"

"It's as all right as it can be for an old woman. These doctors only know how to do one thing and that's give people pills. They give you a pill for everything, even to make you sleep." She paused. "I don't take them on because, if you do, you'll go crazy before you get sick. Now, what's so important that you sent my grandson away from me?"

I put my head down on the table; not wanting to look at her. "In the next few days, a lot of things will be happening in my life. If everything goes as planned, life will be great and I'll be able to get out from my present situation."

"I told you not to marry that girl. But I hope you're not going to do anything stupid to get out of it."

"Grandma, only time will tell whether or not what I'm about to do is stupid. An opportunity has presented itself and I'm going to try and take advantage of it. If things don't work out, I've left a letter in your mailbox with a bank card with both of our names on it. It'll enable you to live the rest of your life in a comfortable manner."

"Son, you know you and Emerald are all I have left and I pray that God takes me away before He does either one of you. While I can't tell you what to do with your life, I want you to think about the people who love you. Whatever happens to you will create a void that will never be filled." Grandma reached out to hold my hand. "I supported you with your father and I will support you for the rest of my life, but be careful. I don't need anything but you and my grandson."

"I know, Mama, but in life sometimes you have to do something to get out of the pits. Otherwise, you'll spend your life asking, 'What if?' I don't want a life full of regrets. This is an opportunity for me to do what Donald wants to do. It's a time for me to be responsible for my future. Like I said, only time will decide whether or not it was a mistake or the best thing I've ever done. I promise to be careful and I know that you'll be there for me. Believe me, it helps a lot." My eyes teared up as I surveyed the wrinkles on her face. She had been through a lot of wars and now she had to wait for the result of yet another one. "Grandma, I'm going to make you proud."

"Son, you've already made me proud in more ways than one. Every time that I see you or Emerald, it makes me want to live longer and longer. I realize that you've made some mistakes but you've been a good son to me.

There isn't anything that I want that you wouldn't give to me if I asked for it." My grandmother was shaking.

"But, Mama, you've never asked for anything," I said.

"Because, Son, there isn't anything that I want. I have food on my plate and clothes on my back; tell me what else I could ask for," she said. "Except for asking the Lord to guide and protect you two. This is it for me, Son. I'm on the final leg of my visit and you and Emerald have made it a wonderful experience."

There wasn't much more to be said. In my grandmother's eyes I saw the confidence that had kept me strong for so many years. I got up and went over to her chair. I hugged her and kissed her on the forehead. "Thanks, Mama."

I spent the rest of the day with Emerald. We went boating; then later in the evening we took in a Broadway play. Even though he enjoyed school and, ordinarily, I wouldn't keep him out for the day, I considered it a worthwhile exception. We can see our past and our future in children, because they are a part of us. My son had my appearance and my heart; his life and his thoughts would shape his entity.

As we sat in the theater enjoying the play, his eyes fixated on the stage, I was overwhelmed with a love that neither time nor man could ever take away. I reached over and hugged and kissed him as he dismissed my intrusion on his entertainment. I sat back in my chair and watched as the actors and actresses put on a repeat performance of what was now routine for them. My life, especially the next few days, would in no part be routine.

I removed the gun from my waistband and dropped it down on Brian's coffee table. "Here's the gun."

Brian picked up the gun expertly and pulled it apart by first dropping the sixteen-chamber magazine in his hand. He cocked the gun, then released the single bullet from the chamber. "I haven't handled one of these in years."

"How does it feel?" I asked, putting the clear, skintight gloves into my pocket.

"Uncle Sam taught me how to kill with weapons so thoughts of death accompany them whenever one is in my hands."

"Well, Brian, I hope there won't be any deaths on this mission because that would mean something went very wrong. If you have to come in gun-blazing, we're all in trouble."

"Do you have the torch?" he asked.

"Yeah, I bought one from Home Depot. I got one with a trigger; there's no time to use a lighter." I watched as Brian put the gun back together. I pulled the gloves that I had worn earlier out of my pocket. "I also got a pair of these gloves."

"You need them with all this CSI shit they have these days. So, you want me to put the gun away now?"

"Naw, let me hold it. I have to meet with my father-in-law and I don't know what will happen," I lied.

Brian gave the gun back to me and I returned it to my waistband.

"When are you meeting with him?"

"Tomorrow, but he doesn't know that yet," I said. "I plan to surprise him."

"Donald, I can't wait for this to be over. Julie doesn't want to have anything to do with me until we finish this. Did she tell you anything?" Brian asked.

"Julie and I only talk about the robbery. I think she wants to make sure everything goes as planned. I've never seen her so focused. Once this is over, I'm sure she'll be back to normal."

I started walking toward the door. I had gotten what I had come for. It was a little bit of insurance. In dealing with thieves, the only thing that could hurt you was trust. Trusting a thief was like believing a politician when it came down to the nuts and bolts. They would put your nuts in their bolts and tighten them. My cell phone rang and I signaled Brian to be quiet as I picked up.

"What's up, Donna?" I adjusted the phone to my ear. I was expecting Donna's call because she had to give me the keys to the handcuffs. I made arrangements to meet with her at Footprints, a small restaurant in Brooklyn and then I hung up the phone.

"Everything good?" Brian asked.

"Yeah, everything is on schedule," I said as I walked out the door.

"Where do you find all these little West Indian restaurants?" Donna asked as she took a seat opposite me. It was 2:30 in the afternoon. The restaurant was empty because it was in between crowds.

"I'm always hunting for food in the evening so I keep asking around for new restaurants to try. I have a lawyer friend who lives in these restaurants. He got married a few years ago so maybe it's not such a hot spot for him anymore. He said that Brooklyn is the only borough that has more West Indian restaurants than Chinese," I said as the waitress brought us glasses of water.

The waitress was a young, white woman. I looked at her and wondered if she was bound by the sins of her father, and maybe her grandfather, for the infliction of slavery. Maybe in a quest to rid herself of that burden, she had come to ask for forgiveness from Blacks by resorting to servitude. We all had our burdens to carry.

"Would you like to see the menu?" she asked.

"No, give us a few minutes," Donna replied. She watched the waitress disappear in the back of the restaurant, then she slid the key over to me. It was a small gold key that I quickly put into my pocket.

I looked over at Donna, a woman who could have been my wife if it weren't for life's circumstances. "You're a beautiful woman."

"But that's not good enough for you, huh, Donald," she whispered with a twinge of anger in her tone. "You added more bricks to the wall once I arrived."

She was right. A beautiful woman could hold the key to many souls and, if kept too long in her grasp, those souls became wandering hollow shells. "Donna, I've been down your road too many times to get trapped in your web. Isn't it enough that our bodies twist and turn in different directions as we give in to the pleasures of the flesh? We can't dance into eternity together because we'll both get engulfed."

"And there, Donald, lies the essence of life. I don't know if your thoughts of me were blinded by our passion. I have no problem with you wanting to be with someone else, but don't act like I'm garbage." Donna reached over the table and as our faces stood inches apart, she added, "The one you turn your back on may be the only one who can save you."

"Donna, let's not get all excited over nothing. You want me to fuck you, that can be arranged, but not until after we do the job. This is new to me and I don't need pussy clouding my mind."

She slid a white card with a magnetic strip toward me. "Here, Room 515 at the Marriott."

"What's that for?"

"We both need to work our stress out."

Donna was good, but I was no amateur. She wanted to control me the way she had controlled all the men and women in her life. I took the card and twirled it around in my right hand. The waitress came over for the second time and we placed our orders.

After she left, I took the card and gave it back to Donna. "Not today."

"Is she a blonde, brunette or down-home chocolate-looking sister?"

Donna was on a fishing expedition in the deep blue sea and right now nothing was biting.

"How is the family?" I asked.

Donna continued the piercing of my soul with her eyes. "They're good. The bills are paid. We make love regularly and we hope to be together for the next twenty years."

"Twenty years is a long time."

"Yeah, well, you know, when the beauty fades, the companionship is what we take with us. Is that what you're looking for Donald; companionship?"

Like every woman who had come before her, Donna wanted to make me a conquest. They wanted to look at me and say out loud or in hushed tones, "This brother is mine." The same thing she had said about her husband and her boss. *Come, puppy, here is your feeding for the day.* "Give it up, Donna; not all mountains are meant to be climbed. And if you try, the consequences can be deadly."

"Here we go, guys. Enjoy." The waitress placed our food before us. I immediately started to eat. Donna bowed her head in a silent prayer before taking up her fork. Needless to say there was no more talk about the direction I had chosen to take with my life.

"Hi." Her voice was soft and sensuous. It was like a voice I had never heard before.

My right hand held the phone tightly to my ear. "What's up?"

"I miss you." She paused before continuing. "What have you been up to?"

I didn't know the right answers to give. "Been trying to tie up some loose ends. The nights are long and there's a craving in my heart, but soon it'll all be over."

"Donald, I know you said that you wanted us to wait until all this is over before a decision is made, but I can't." I could hear the trembling in her voice. "What I feel for you is a once-in-a-lifetime thing and I want you to know that."

I switched the phone from my right ear to my left. I wanted to be with her right then but I resisted the temptation. "There are no guarantees."

There was a hesitation before she said, "I realize that there will never be any guarantees. Life is about uncertainty and change. What looks good today could make you walk on the other side of the street and see tomorrow in disgust. Donald, I want the moment; fuck the season."

"You cursed," I said.

"Yeah, get over it. I do many things you don't know about."

I laughed; her truths were my ignorance. "Yeah, you've got me on that one. Love is like a soccer ball. It gets kicked around all over the place until someone scores; then it becomes an irreplaceable trophy. People are then willing to pay up to a million dollars for it."

"Or twenty million," she added, bringing the conversation back to our reality.

I didn't feel like discussing the robbery that day. "You had to remind me."

"Yes, I did, because our lives depend on it. Where we go from here is dependent on what happens in two days. Donald, I'm not going to be a kept woman. I want to be your wife. I want us to have a child in celebration of our love. Emerald is such a wonderful boy. Don't you think he needs a sister?"

"I've thought about it."

"Just thought about it?" The disappointment in her voice made the phone seem heavy.

"Julie, please don't question my love for you. I have a lot of things on my mind. Some of it I can't discuss with you. You know my life is complicated and the things I've done and I'm going to do will change my life forever. And it might not be in a good way," I said. Julie's being in my life for the past few days had started to wear heavily on me.

"Donald, what happened to the times when you would tell me everything? Isn't our love based on friendship? Now you're making me feel like an outsider; untrustworthy. I don't like that feeling. Hold on; Brian is on the line."

She clicked the phone over and I was left in silence. To protect Julie, I had to limit her information. I couldn't tell her of my plans for Malcolm or the situation at home with Lauren. There was a beep on my phone and I looked at the incoming number. It was Malcolm. I had left a message for him to call me back.

"Yeah, Malcolm," I said, knowing that he would be irritated with the way I was speaking to him.

The irritation was clearly evident in his voice. "I thought our next conversation would be the conclusion of our deal."

"There's been a change in plans. I'm leaving this place tomorrow night."

"You're picking up and leaving your child behind." He sounded skeptical.

I paused before answering, making him think that his words were affecting me. "Do you have the money for me?"

"But I didn't complete my part of the deal," he said. "I was planning to take care of Annette in a couple of days."

"I'm not concerned about you taking care of Annette. You have no choice in the matter. She will not let your daughter have another child for me. So, if you want your granddaughter, you'll have to take care of Annette. I'm not doing this twice. Once was terrible enough. Will you have the money tomorrow?"

Malcolm paused for a second. "I could have it by the evening. But you won't get it until I receive all the signed paperwork."

"The paperwork is already signed, Malcolm."

"So what happened, Donald? She wants you to leave New York and start a family someplace else?"

"Malcolm, it's none of your fucking business why I do what I do. Just meet me by the park around eleven and bring all my money. Hopefully, that'll be the last time we see each other."

The phone clicked again as Julie hung up, probably in frustration.

"I'll see you tomorrow," Malcolm said and hung up the phone.

I dialed Julie's number and waited for her to pick up. She picked up after the fifth ring. "What's up with Brian?"

"He isn't happy. He wanted to come over."

"Is he coming over?" I asked, not sure that I wanted an answer.

"Donald, how could you ask me something like that?" The anger was evident in her voice.

"Julie, I had to ask."

"Donald, I don't know what your opinion of me is, but it was enough that I had to go from Brian to you. I've never had two men in one year, much less slept with two men at the same time. I haven't been with Brian since I've been with you and I doubt I'll ever be with him again."

"Julie, it's just the life that I have lived. I usually have to ask these questions." It was comical that Julie had said that she hadn't slept with two men in one year. I had personally slept with more than five women in a week. It was our difference and our strength. Julie and I were on the same planet but, even though we both lived in New York, our days and nights were not the same. Did a person's environment shape him or did he shape his environment? I didn't know. There were so many people whose lives might have been worse or better than mine, yet their directions were drastically different from mine.

The anger was still in her voice. "Donald, I'll speak with you tomorrow."

I thought about saying something to make her feel better but it might have backfired and made it worse. "Okay," I said and hung up the phone.

I dialed Brian's number to make arrangements to meet him.

"What's up, Brian?" I asked when he came on the phone.

"I don't know what's going on with Julie. I don't know what to do. She doesn't want me to come over. She won't even call me unless I call her. Donald, I think I've lost her. You're her friend. She hasn't told you anything?"

"Not a damn thing," I said. "Brian, why don't you give her some time? Sometimes you have to let a woman go for her to come back to you."

"Yeah. I know that one and if she doesn't come back, hunt her down and shoot her," he said as muffled laughter came over the phone.

"Well, I wasn't thinking of that extreme, but I guess that would work, providing you're willing to go to jail over some pussy."

"Donald, there you go again, thinking of women as pieces of meat. If you ever really fall in love, I'm sure that your opinion will change."

"Maybe you're right, Brian, but I believe my grandmother when she said whenever that happens I will be fucked. But, like you said, maybe I need to."

"You are finally listening! Donald, in this world of trials and tribulations, love is the only thing we've got. Now, I'm begging you, please talk to Julie. I need to know what's going on," he pleaded.

If there was a place for sinners and liars, I needed to be first in line. "I hear you, Brian. I promise I'll talk to her tomorrow. And I'll see you tomorrow to return the thing."

"See you tomorrow," Brian said and hung up the phone.

I reached into the closet with a napkin and took the gun with two magazines and put it in a black shoulder bag. I had to get to the park at least two hours ahead of the meeting. When we had left the park the first time, I had made a note of where Malcolm was parked. With humans being creatures of habit, I was certain that he would park there again. I knew he would not bring any of his guards with him; he did not perceive me as a physical threat. I was going to make sure that was the last mistake he ever made. I was a man and I was capable of killing, just like him.

CHAPTER 19
2ND DAY

I walked into the church a few minutes after the service had started. The scent of incense permeated the air. I had accepted the fact that I was beautiful and wherever I went women's eyes would zoom in on me like bees to a hive. I ignored their lustful eyes in the church of the Lord and took a seat between a young boy dressed in a baby-blue suit and a young woman in a red and white dress. Her ample bosom was uplifted by the currently popular Wonderbra. She smiled; certain that she had won a prize. I smiled back in acknowledgment that we happened to be at the same place at the same time. The young boy, who could not have been more than six years old, nudged me to direct my attention to his mother; a woman whose best days had long passed. I returned her joyful smile, then directed my attention to the front of the church.

The pastor, an old white man in his late sixties, had a lot to say about the weakness in our characters. He called on his parishioners to leave the sex, drugs and meanness alone. He urged us to love each other and help each other. There were a lot of amens muttered in the church as each main point was acknowledged. I agreed with everything he had to say, including the fact that we were totally self-obsessed with our pitiful appearance. Throughout the service, I was aware of the closing of space between the lady in red and white and myself, until her ample chest was resting comfortably on my arm.

The service continued into a series of announcements and information decimation. After fifteen minutes of preaching and an hour and forty-five minutes of church affairs, the service was finally over.

The lady in red had a name. "My name is Cindi."

"Donald." I stood and waited for her to do the same. She didn't seem like she was in a hurry to go anywhere. The six-year-old boy had shimmied himself out and was now waiting for his mother at the end of the pew.

"Excuse me," the boy's mother said to me, her smile no longer visible. It had been replaced with an angry scowl that begged for an explanation of my audacity in keeping her from her appointed task.

"Cindi, we're blocking the pew," I said.

Cindi looked over at the restless mother, rolling her eyes, and continued to rummage through her red bag. "I've got it," she said, pulling out a red phone. She then stood up and walked out of the pew. I followed behind her with the now irate mother behind me. I stopped outside of the pew to glance at my watch. I had come to the church to go to confessional. It was my minor bid at salvation. The capacity-filled church was now inhabited by a sprinkling of people. I was about to head to the confessional booth when Cindi blocked my way.

"You weren't going to leave before saying bye and taking my number, were you?" She pushed her hips back to accentuate her big, fat ass.

I reached out my hand and took her hand and shook it firmly. "Cindi, it was a pleasure meeting you. I must go."

"You're married, aren't you?" she asked.

"Yes, very happily married," I said.

"So, can we be friends?" she asked, not losing that "you're mine" look on her face.

I put my left hand over my eyes and appeared to be in deep thought. "I don't think my wife would like that." I made my way toward the confessional booth without waiting for a response from Cindi.

In direct contrast to the big open church, the confessional booth was cramped and smelled of wilted flowers. I did the customary kneeling, then took a seat next to the porous screen. A small scraping sound indicated the priest was sliding his screen back.

"I'm sorry, Father, for I have sinned," I said.

There was an outline of a man's face behind the screen. "What have you done, my son?"

"Where should I begin, dear father?"

"Wherever you wish, my son."

"Well, Father, I have slept with hundreds of women, lied to men and women and cheated on my wife on numerous occasions. I got married to my wife because she had money and hated my father because he raped my mother. I killed my father and I see no end in sight for my horrible behavior."

"Why are you here, my son?" the priest asked.

"Father, I have recently fallen in love with a beautiful woman whom I would like to spend the rest of my life with. But my lust for the flesh seems to be a never-ending battle. I've been good lately but I don't know how long I can continue. Later on today, I have to settle a matter that will free my body but tie up my soul. And tomorrow will mark a total change in the direction of my life."

As I spoke to the priest, I began to feel much more relaxed and the words came out effortlessly as the tremor in my hands subsided.

"Son, listen to that guide that God has given you and follow it. If your guide is telling you that it is wrong, do not do it. Your past sins can only be forgiven by your prayers and the direction of your future. Pray to the Lord for guidance so that the little voice will steer you away from the bad. Pray to the Lord so that little voice will stop you before your misdeeds. Son, you have done bad deeds but God has welcomed worse into His garden. Go forth today and be blessed." He pulled the screen back and only his presence was felt behind the screen.

"Thank you, Father," I said and rose from the wooden bench. I walked out of the booth, relieved that I was no longer the only one weighted by my troubles. I half expected to see Cindi rising from one of the pews. I was happy when I walked outside in the company of myself. I didn't know what I was hoping to find in church, but I felt I had to tell my tale. I knew that there wouldn't be any intervention by God to change my actions, yet I was drawn by the only savior of man. As I walked down the street toward my car, I realized that only man could stop himself. There was no lightning bolt that would come crashing down from the sky and leave me in a molten heap. I had escaped the punishment of God and now I had to continue to create my reality.

The sun had made its descent about an hour ago and the cool fall warranted a light jacket. I parked my car on 88th Street, a driveway away from Seaview Avenue. There were lots of parking spaces on Seaview Avenue, the street that bordered the park with the Atlantic Ocean, but I didn't park my car anyplace on that street. It was like going to fuck a man's wife and parking in his driveway, which was a no-no. In the event of a quick getaway, there should be some maneuvering possible. While in the car, I had slipped the gun into my waistband and it was now nudging against my bare skin. I took it and a small pillow to the arranged meeting place. I threw the pillow a few feet away from where our meeting was supposed to be held.

I went into the park and did a few stretches. There were about two other people running in the park. I watched one of them speed by me as if he was about to catch a moving bus. The other was a woman in her late fifties; her pace on the track meant that time was not of the essence to her. She was most likely of the opinion that whenever you finished, it was a good thing. The hood was over my head as I started the jog around the park. The increase in the air pressure felt good as my heart pumped blood through my body. The gun nudging against my skin was becoming unbearable. I made it around the park twice, then I jogged off the track to wait for the arrival of Mr. Malcolm. As expected, he was punctual, parking his black 2006 Chrysler 300 behind a black Mazda 626. I watched him get out of the car with a black bag. He adjusted his black slacks, then started the trek across the park. He had a fedora pulled down over his eyes. I waited for him to go to the arranged meeting place before I started walking over to join him.

I removed the gun as I walked down the small path that led to the clearing. I saw Mr. Malcolm ahead of me; his face turned in the opposite direction.

"I see you made it," I said, hoping not to spook him.

"Yes, I have it all here for you," he said, still facing away from me.

I picked up the pillow and put it in front of the gun. I moved swiftly toward Mr. Malcolm, my finger on the trigger. As I approached, he began to turn around. I reached forward with both hands, my left hand holding the pillow and my right hand, the gun. The blood circulated in my body three times as fast as when I was running earlier. As soon as I made contact against him with the pillow, I jammed the gun into it and pulled the trigger. My hand jerked as three bullets left the barrel of the gun and Mr. Malcolm pitched forward. In his right hand, he was clutching a forty-five pistol; definitely a relic from his younger days. He had fallen forward on his face with his mouth and eyes wide open. I reached down and disengaged his fingers from the black bag he was carrying. I unzipped the bag and opened it to find a bag full of torn newspapers. I smiled because my prediction had come true. I went through the bag, then later his pockets. I removed his wallet and his keys. I made one last look around the area, then exited the parking lot in the opposite direction from where I had come in.

It took me a minute to make the complete circle back to my car. I got in and drove off. It took me about two minutes to get onto the Belt Parkway; then I exited to a rest area overlooking the sea. I got out of the car and ignored the couple humping in a white Toyota Camry. I walked out to the water and under the cover of the night, I threw Mr. Malcolm's belongings into Jamaica Bay. I lashed out with my right hand to crush a mosquito that had made preparation to use my neck for dinner. The small red blotch of blood was barely visible in the center of my palm. The mosquito, like me, was trying to survive and in the process it had lost its life. I had begun the cleansing and whereas it wasn't as spiritual as in BLACKFUNK, nevertheless, I hoped it would be equally as effective. Sometimes you had to start anew and only take what you couldn't leave behind. I was on my way to that new start.

I drove to Brian's apartment, being ever so obedient to the driving laws of our city. Brian was waiting for me at the door when I reached out to knock on it.

"You took care of your business?" he asked as he let me into his apartment.

"Yeah, I had to show the old man that I wasn't going to be a punk anymore," I said, handing Brian the bag with the gun.

"I feel you, my brother. Sometimes, when they don't listen to the words, the sword has to be brandished."

I laughed at Brian's attempt at being poetic. "Brian, you've been reading the spoken word?"

"No, Man, these guys aren't saying anything new. You want one?"

"No, I don't feel like alcohol this evening. I want something much lighter. Do you have any orange juice or lemonade?"

Brian paused for a second. "Yeah, I have some orange juice. Foodtown had it on sale, two for five, so I picked up a couple. You don't think the old man will bother you anymore?"

"No, Man, we came to an understanding today. He now realizes how much I love my son. I don't think I'll need to have another conversation with him. You heard from Julie?"

"Yeah, she surprised me and gave me a call today. I was totally shocked. Nothing has changed though. She told me that she'll talk to me tomorrow."

"I hope you've been taking care of yourself. Now is the time to dip into that black book." I took the glass of orange juice from Brian.

"I tried, Man, but I couldn't do it. I had this girl, Niki, over last night. You know, the emergency fuck, but I couldn't go through with it. She's cool though. She told me to call her whenever." Brian sat down at the table, opposite me, with a Heiny in his hand.

"Well, a lot of things will be decided tomorrow. I think I'm going to go home and get some sleep." I drank the rest of the orange juice.

"You nervous about tomorrow?" Brian asked.

"I thought I was going to be, but I'm not. I guess the shit I've been going through has created a certain resolve in my mind."

"Don't start acting like President Bush and go and start another war. I get very concerned when the word 'resolve' starts getting thrown around."

"Brian, you're an idiot," I said, getting up from the table.

"We'll talk tomorrow," Brian said as I walked to the door. I had one more stop to make before I went home.

"You didn't expect me?" I stepped into the house and closed the door.

Julie walked ahead of me into the living room. "I wanted to talk to you but I didn't know if I should call."

"I just left Brian's apartment." I took a seat on the couch.

"He told me that you had taken the gun. What did you do with the gun?"

"I had some cleaning to do," I said.

"You're not going to tell me what you did with the gun?"

"If I do, it might create trouble for you," I said.

"What do you think could be worse for me, knowing or not knowing? You used to tell me when your shit came out black. Now it's on a need-to-know basis. Just because you got between my legs, now I can't be trusted." Julie had begun to raise her voice.

"It's not that, Julie. If anything happens to me, I don't want you to take the fall with me. I want to protect you."

"That's a whole lot of bullshit, Donald. If trouble is going to come our way I need to know where it will be coming from. As you can see, I'm not as innocent as you seem to think. I can handle a lot more than you give me credit for. I handled your dick, didn't I?"

I smiled as my loins began to stir. "Come over here!"

As Julie walked toward me, I was once more caught up in her rapture. I wanted to feel the warmth of her womanhood. I needed to be inside of her. She came to me and stuck her tongue into my mouth and I held onto it for dear life. I pulled her shorts down to find out that the strings that she was wearing to cover her womanhood had come off with her shorts. I lifted her up and put her on the table quickly, unbuttoning my pants to free my now erect penis. As I pushed her back away from the edge of the table, I got up onto one of the table's five chairs. I opened her legs wide and, with my feet on the chair, I plunged into her, savoring her wetness. As she screamed for me to give it to her, I plunged in and out of her as the crescendo of pleasure for me was reached with ten strokes. The contents of my now deflated penis lay within her.

I sat down on the chair that I had used to mount her, my jeans at the heels of my feet.

"What did you do with the gun?" Julie sat on the table next to me, her legs swinging back and forth.

I lifted my head up to make eye contact with her. "I shot Malcolm to death."

Julie kept looking at me. Then she spoke very softly. "Was it an accident?"

"Yes," I said. "I was trying to scare him but he tried to take the gun away from me and it went off."

"It's obvious that you didn't call the police. That was very smart of you."

"If I had, tomorrow would never be."

"Exactly. Did anyone see you?"

"I doubt it. It was late in the park. Everyone is scared of the park at night; unless it's a person walking a dog. Some people care more about their pets than their own safety."

Julie came over and stood behind my chair. "Everything will be okay, Donald. After tomorrow, everything will fall into place."

I reached out and put my hands around her waist. "Yeah, tomorrow we start over."

I awoke to the birds chirping on the lawn outside. I had left Julie's house around two in the morning after she had given me a much needed blow job. The exploits of the evening had evaporated all my energy and the comforts of my bed sent me into REM as soon as my head hit the pillow. I woke up and went into the shower. When I got out of the shower, my son had taken residence on my bed.

"What's up, Son?" I asked, walking by the bed on my way to the closet.

"Grandma called and asked if anyone had seen Granddad," he said.

"Did you see him?" I asked, taking out a pair of jeans and a shirt from my closet.

"No. Do you think she still wants me to come over there after school?" Emerald asked.

"I'm sure she does. Phillip, her driver, is picking you up, right?"

"Yep, Grandma said she'll come with him. That means we'll stop and get ice cream." Emerald was smiling.

I zipped up my jeans. "Don't eat too much ice cream; you might get a belly-ache. I'll pick you up from Grandma's around nine and will take you on a surprise trip."

"Where are we going?" Emerald asked.

"If I told you, then it wouldn't be a secret, would it?" I lifted him up into my arms.

"I guess so," he said.

"Do you know how much I love you?" I said, kissing him on the cheek.

"A lot." He had a beautiful smile on his face.

"Yes, my son, a whole lot. Now go with your mommy." I put him back down on the ground.

He ran out of the room. "See you later, Dad. I love you."

I left my suit in the car as I walked into a small Jamaican restaurant named McKenzie's on Avenue L in Brooklyn. As usual, the seating part of the restaurant was empty but there was a line for takeout. I went up to the counter and ordered a small oxtail dinner. I waited for the young woman to give me the food; then I took it back to a booth. As soon as I had put down the food, my cell phone rang. I looked at the number. It was a number I hadn't seen before. When I answered, Donna was on the other end.

I separated a small piece of fat from the oxtail. "Yeah, Donna. Any changes?"

"No, everything is on schedule. Don't forget to make eye contact with Kathleen before you move in. Once you're finished, we'll meet under the bridge as planned." The excitement was evident in her voice.

"All right; I'll see you later."

I closed the phone and put it down on the table. The next time I expected to hear from Donna was when her boss and Kathleen left the office. At that time, I would be at least a block away from there. The briefcase in the trunk of my car was about five inches larger than a normal briefcase. In a small compartment was a yellow blow torch. In the main compartment was a two-by-four, and the knife and gloves. I picked up the phone and made a conference call to Julie and Brian. I finished eating and walked out of the restaurant. I drove back to my house and changed into a dark gray Armani suit. After I left the house I pulled the car into an unused parking lot and put the wig on.

As expected, the business district was almost deserted by 7:30 p.m. A few stragglers in business suits were the only remnants of a city that had tens of thousands of people on the streets about five hours ago. I had parked my car about a half-mile away from the Atlantic Avenue train station in Brooklyn. There were plenty of parking spaces available on the street after five-thirty, unlike early in the morning when you had to get downtown by seven-thirty to get a spot. The walk to the train station was uneventful; with the exception of a few young white women giving me the once-over. I felt flattered by their attention but the timing wasn't right. Ten minutes after getting into the train station, I was on my way to Manhattan in a brand-new train.

I walked up and down the street, waiting for the call from Donna. It finally came about twenty minutes later. The street lights had come on to illuminate the business district as I made my way to Edna Street. I walked with confidence but not hurriedly because the human eyes are always attracted to abnormal behavior. I wanted to be another faceless white businessman on his way home from a long day at the office. The plan was for me to be on the opposite side of the street when Kathleen and her husband made their way down the street. There was an old apartment building that was being totally renovated. Donna had identified that building because there was only one bulb illuminating an entrance about twenty feet in length. It was there that I was going to make my move. I waited at the opposite end of the street from where Kathleen and Peter would be coming. The old apartment building was about thirty feet from me.

Kathleen looked stunning in a short, black, formfitting dress. As she walked with Peter, the joyful look on her face reflected a woman in total bliss. She saw me as soon as she turned onto the block and took her husband's spare hand and laid it on her butt. He squeezed her ass as she stuck her tongue into his ear. I could only imagine what she was saying to him. The plan was for Donna to crush a Viagra pill and slip it into his drink before Kathleen arrived for a surprise visit. The Viagra pill was to ensure that pleasure came before responsibility. Peter knew what he was carrying and he knew what would happen to him if he fucked up.

I watched them coming down the street, Kathleen all over her husband, rubbing the front of his pants and kissing on his ear. When they reached the front of the building that was being renovated, Kathleen turned her husband around as I walked down the street until I was directly opposite them. I had confidence in Kathleen that she would not allow Peter to turn around. She pulled on Peter's free hand as she tried to entice him to go into the passageway. I stood there, looking around, a few droplets of sweat coming down my forehead. Finally, pleasure overruled responsibility and Peter followed his wife into the passageway. I quickly walked across the street and before I entered the darkness of the passageway, I had the two-by-four in my hand. I walked slowly and quietly. I heard groans before I was able to see Peter, his back to me and his pants down to his ankles. The briefcase was hanging loosely from his hand by the gold handcuffs. From experience, I knew that Kathleen was a pro and my dick started to harden thinking about what she could do to me.

I lifted the two-by-four and came down hard on the side of Peter's head. He crumpled to the ground. I knelt down and quickly unlocked Peter's handcuffs. I deposited the briefcase into mine and took out the blow torch.

"Before you do that, give me the gloves and the knife," Kathleen said. I gave her the gloves, which she quickly put on, then I gave her the knife. "Step back."

I did what I was told.

Kathleen lifted the knife up high, brought it down into her husband's back and then threw the knife onto the ground.

I looked at her emotionless face. There was no joy or anger. It was like she was doing a job that she had done for twenty years; just another day in the trenches.

"The knife." I reached down to pick it up.

"No, leave it," Kathleen said. "If you were smart, your prints won't be on that."

"I was smart," I said.

Kathleen smiled. "You don't think I know that black bitch has been fucking my husband."

"None of my business," I said. "Give me your cell number in case I need to give you the heads-up."

She called it out and I put it directly into my cell phone.

"Sometimes, it only takes one stone to kill two birds. Now hit me," she said.

This time I brought the two-by-four from the side of my waist and smashed it against Kathleen's face. Blood flew out of her mouth. I threw the piece of wood down. She staggered and fell to the ground. I took the blow torch and pulled the trigger. I lifted Peter's right wrist. And while holding his fingers I burnt around his wrist as the smell of burning flesh scorched my nostrils.

"That's enough; leave," Kathleen said, her eyes bloodshot and blood dripping down the side of her face.

Once more I complied. I got up off the ground.

Kathleen wrapped her hand around her husband's head.

I straightened out my suit and dusted off any particles that had gotten on it. I turned around and started to walk toward the light. I looked back briefly to see Kathleen starting to drag herself forward. I moved quickly, knowing that Kathleen would be screaming for help as soon as she dragged herself out to the sidewalk. When I was close to the sidewalk, I looked up and down the now completely deserted street. I made a left turn and walked quickly down the street.

At the end of the street, I saw a yellow cab approaching. I hoped that it was Julie and Brian. She was wearing a turban that made her look like a gorgeous Arab. I opened the back door and got in.

"Where's Brian?" I asked.

"I told him we didn't need him. I've got the gun," she said.

"Give it back to Brian," I said.

"Okay," she said.

I gave Julie the briefcase with Peter's briefcase inside of it.

"How did it go?" she asked.

"Good, with the exception of a twist."

"What happened?"

I didn't feel like talking right then. "I'll tell you later."

"Brian is at my house," she said.

I looked at her eyes in the rearview mirror. "Do what you have to do?"

The ride to Brooklyn was without conversation. My cell phone rang every five minutes. Finally I turned it off. Donna was history.

"Leave me here," I said as she stopped at the corner of Atlantic and Fourth Avenues to the annoyance of the drivers behind her. I got out of the car and walked to my car. In the car, I took off the wig and put it in the briefcase. I had one more thing to do. There was no way in hell that Lauren was going to have another child of mine.

CHAPTER 21
1ST EVENING

I pulled up in front of my house in the darkness of night. I unlocked the front door and stepped into the house. The first person to greet me was Annette.

"I see you're still ugly," I said as I walked by her.

"Stop right there, Motherfucker!" Annette shouted at me.

I continued to walk to the stairs.

"Motherfucker, I said to stop right there before I blow your brains out."

Those words definitely got my attention. I turned around to see that Annette was pointing a nine-millimeter at my head. "What the fuck's wrong with you, Bitch?"

"Just don't move. I'm going to have my fun today." Annette widened her stance to shoulder-width. She flipped her cell phone open and punched in some numbers.

"Who the fuck are you calling?" I asked, getting very angry.

"Should I shoot him now?" she said into the phone.

"Shoot me?" I said incredulously.

"Okay, I'll wait until you come, but if he moves, I'm going to kill him."

She put the phone back into her pocket.

Annette wanted to kill me. I was one hundred percent positive of that. The only person who was saving me was the one who was on his way there.

"Can I sit down?"

"No, Motherfucker, your sitting days are over. The only thing I want to see you do is lie down dead."

The gun in her hand was unwavering.

There was no more conversation until the doorbell rang.

Lauren came running down the stairs. "Is anyone going to answer the door?"

"Bitch, get the door," Annette said to Lauren.

The human body sometimes takes a while to adjust to certain situations. "Annette, what's going on here? Please put the gun away and leave Donald alone." Lauren's eyes were swollen.

"Lauren, don't get me angry. You know what happens when you get me angry. Please go and open the door."

Lauren went over to the door and opened it.

Donna pushed Lauren aside and stepped into the house as if she owned the place.

She came straight over to me, her face contorted in anger. "I told you not to try to fuck me."

"Long time, no see, Donna," I said with a smirk on my face.

"What's going on here?!" Lauren shouted.

"Bitch, shut the fuck up," Annette and Donna said in unison.

"This is theatrical," I said.

"Donald, where is the money?" Donna asked.

"I see you gave Miss Ugly a taste of your pussy and she got hooked," I said.

"Donna, let me shoot his ass now," Annette demanded.

"Annette, you ugly bitch, shut the fuck up and give me that damn gun." Donna stretched her hand out for the gun.

Annette handed the gun over to Donna. "I'm sorry, Donna, but you heard what he said to me."

Lauren had made her way over to Annette. She now stood between Annette and Donna.

Donna started to move toward me with the gun in her hand. "I'm going to shoot you in the kneecaps; then I'm going to work my way up. Donald, what the fuck was going through your mind? You thought that you could play me?"

"I'm sorry, Donna, but my wife and I slept together because we wanted another child. I had too much on my mind."

Annette turned blue or whatever color black people turned when they were angry. She grabbed Lauren by the throat. "Bitch, you slept with him and you're pregnant."

Lauren started to cry. "I'm sorry. I'm so sorry, Annette."

I brought my hands back and started to push my waist forward in a jerking motion.

"I fucked her good, too. You should've been there, Annette. I guarantee you that we'll have a daughter in eight months."

Annette held Lauren up by the throat with one hand as she brought her other hand up with the force of anger and hate. She repeatedly punched Lauren in the stomach until blood started to ooze from Lauren's mouth. She let go of Lauren and Lauren fell down to the floor.

"You bitches are…"

Donna had turned around to see the action between Lauren and Annette and that gave me the opportunity I needed. I leapt across the floor, crossing the space between Donna and me within mere seconds. I grabbed the gun from Donna's hand as my hand descended on her mouth, sending a tooth flying out of her mouth. Donna's body crumpled to the floor.

"You motherfucker!" Annette screamed as she jumped onto my back, grabbing my hand that held the gun and shaking it. I tried to throw her off my back, but she held on tightly to my neck. I started to spin her round and round but she held on even tighter.

"You killed my daughter!" Lauren screamed.

For me to turn around to face the lunging Lauren would require at least a few seconds. It was time I didn't have.

"What the…" It was all I heard from Annette, then the hold she had on my neck was no more. Slowly, she slid off my back onto the floor. I turned around and there Lauren stood with a bloody, nine-inch knife in her hand. Annette lay on the ground, her eyes opened wide but vacant, blood flowing freely down her back. The knife had penetrated her back and gone through her heart.

I put the gun into my waistband. "I'm leaving."

Lauren looked at me as if she was seeing me for the first time. "You really didn't want me to have your child, did you?"

I shook my head. "There's enough pain in this world. We don't need to bring more. We were blessed with Emerald. I think that's enough. Do you want me to take them out of here?"

Lauren shook her head. "No, by the time Donna wakes up, the knife will be in her hand. I learned a lot from my father."

"I'm taking Emerald," I said.

"Do that, because I have some issues to resolve, but once I'm okay, I will want my son."

"I won't keep him from you," I said.

"You know my father won't allow it," she said.

I walked toward the door and turned the knob. "I will deal with that when the time comes."

"Tell him that I love him," she said.

"I'll do that. Take care of yourself." I opened the door and walked out without looking back.

"The cops are looking for Malcolm," Dora said as I put Emerald into the car.

"I hope they find him." I shut the car door. I felt sorry for Dora. She looked like death had approached her door.

"He's never done anything like this," she said. "I hope he's all right."

"Good night, Dora," I said.

"Daddy, are we going home?" Emerald asked.

"No, Son, we're going to meet Aunty Julie." I picked up the phone and dialed Julie's cell number. The call went straight to voice mail. I hung up and tried her home number. The answering machine came on. I stepped on the accelerator.

"Where is Aunty Julie?" Emerald asked.

"She's at home, Son. Go to sleep," I said.

"Okay, Daddy," Emerald said, the weariness evident in his voice.

There were no cars in Julie's driveway so I pulled up in it. The lights were out in the house. I left Emerald asleep in the car and walked to the front door. On the handle of the front door, there was a white bag with my name on it. I slipped the bag off the doorknob. I looked into the bag and my gun was in it with a note. She had left the porch light on so I took the note out and read it.

Love is never easy but you make it extremely hard. Brian and I are going to try to start over so we must leave. The keys to the house are underneath the front mat. In the house, you will find five million dollars. I hope it will be enough for you and Emerald, to start over. Donald, please remember that I do love you but I will never be able to trust you. And the things you have done lately have started me wondering what kind of man are you. I don't want to be looking over my shoulder for the rest of my life. Please take care of yourself and Emerald and thanks for everything.

Love, Julie

I put the gun in my waistband, ripped the paper in small pieces and littered the lawn with it. I got back into the car. My grandmother had warned me and I hadn't listened. Now the punishment was being dealt.

"Where is Aunty Julie?" Emerald asked as I started the car.

I didn't know that he had awakened. "She's dead, my son. She's as good as dead."

"I love you, Daddy," Emerald said.

"I love you too, Son. I really do." He was my lifeline.

I looked back at him and he was fast asleep. I doubt he even heard what I had said. I squeezed the steering wheel until the veins popped out all over my hands. I was hurting but I was going to be all right. I was close to being a pimp but now I was back to being a whore. Only this time, I had a lot more experience. I had blood all over my hands and I was about to get even bloodier. Julie and Brian were on their way to hell and I was going to make sure that I was the one giving directions. I pulled up in front of the Marriott at eleven-thirty. I let them valet park my car as I lifted Emerald onto my shoulders. The young woman at the desk looked me over like I had kidnapped my son. I didn't say anything; instead I presented my American Express card.

I put Emerald down on the bed and went to the mini-bar. I took out a few small bottles of liquor. I mixed them together, and then added some Pepsi to the mixture. The night was still young and I had some thinking to do.

I was hurting, not because Julie had taken fifteen million dollars away from me but because she had taken my heart. I squeezed my eyes to stop thinking about her. She had gotten into a place where no woman had set foot before. Once more my eyes became bloodshot as Julie's knife diced my heart up. I didn't know if I could have been a hundred percent faithful to her but I was going to try. I didn't know if my love for her was going to last a month but I was going to try to make it last a lifetime.

"Fuck the money," I said out loud.

I had no need for the money she had left in the house so I didn't take it. I was in pain and the night did nothing to stop the bleeding.

I sat up looking out the window at Brooklyn Bridge as the time started to count from one. It wasn't until four that I kissed Emerald on the cheek and lay down next to him to rest my weary body. Tomorrow I was going to tie up all the loose ends and maybe the whore would finally get off my back.

CHAPTER 23
EPILOGUE

I got up at eight in the morning and grabbed my phone from the night table. I looked at Emerald who was still fast asleep. I went to the address book and pulled up Kathleen's number. I dialed it.

"Hello." She sounded drowsy.

"How are you doing?" I asked.

"My husband and I will live but he's crippled for life."

"Did they catch the person who did it?"

"No, but the police are investigating."

"I need a number for one of your husband's friends."

"What for?" she asked.

"Something was taken from me." I was banking on her believing that Donna had double-crossed me.

"Is it her?"

"Yes," I said.

"I'll send it to you." She hung up the phone.

A few seconds passed before I received a text message with a number.

"Daddy, where are we going today?" my son asked.

I turned around to see him sitting up in bed, still rubbing his eyes.

"Well, your daddy has to do something; then we're going home."

"But I thought we were going on a trip," he said.

"We are, but we have to get Mommy first."

"Okay, where are we going?"

"Come here, Little Boy." I stretched my hands out to him. He came running and I lifted him up into my arms. "Wherever you want to go."

"Disneyland!"

I kissed him on the cheek. "Then we're going to Disneyland."

I canvassed the sidewalk with my eyes as I looked for a public phone, finally finding one on the corner of Third Avenue. I told Emerald, "I'll be right back."

I dropped two quarters into the coin slot and was rewarded with a dial tone. I dialed the cell phone number that Kathleen had given me.

"Hello." The voice on the other end had a European accent, from which country I didn't know.

"Listen," I said. "I will only say this once."

"Who are you?"

"There was a robbery yesterday on Park Avenue. I know who did it."

The voice became a little bit more excited. "I'm listening."

"You will find five million in saving bonds from the robbery in a house in Queens. The address is 1020 USA Avenue. The owner and her man have the rest of the money."

"Where are they?" the voice asked.

"I'm giving you the pussy; now you want the lubricant too? Find them your fucking self." I hung up the phone.

I pulled into my driveway twenty-five minutes later and Emerald was out of the car and at the front door in seconds. Lauren opened the door with a surprised expression on her face.

She picked him up and kissed him, her face basking in joy. I walked toward the door. She was still standing there but Emerald was gone.

"My father's dead," Lauren announced with very little sadness in her voice. "The police left a few minutes ago but they will be back. I told them that I came home and found Donna and Annette on the floor. I told them that Annette was my lover."

"Did they believe you?"

"For now they do. I will let our lawyers deal with the cops. What are you doing back here?"

"I'm sorry to hear about your father. I'm back here because this is my house." I stood opposite her, the door still open. "From now on, there won't be any bitches coming in my house. If you want some pussy, feel free to go to a hotel or do whatever, but don't bring them here. This is my fucking house and if you don't like it, you can leave right now."

"My mom wants you to help her with my father's burial arrangements."

"When is the funeral?"

"Sunday afternoon."

"Tell your mom that I'll be there tomorrow. Do they have any idea who killed your father?" I asked, my hand still on the front door.

"No, but we all knew that my father dealt with some shady characters. His violent death isn't totally unexpected. We always knew that one day it would catch up with him. The cops think it was a deal gone bad."

"I never had a good relationship with your father but death is always sad."

Lauren looked upstairs in the direction of Emerald's room. "Emerald will take it very hard. He loved his grandfather."

"Yeah, I know, there will be a lot of tears on Sunday afternoon." My cell phone began to ring.

She looked directly into my unwavering eyes. "I'm going to make something for Emerald. Do you want anything?"

"A sandwich would be good."

"Okay." Lauren walked toward the kitchen.

I looked at the number on the phone. I flipped the phone open.

"What's up, Brenda?"

"I'm giving you another chance to go away with me," she said.

"Any day after Sunday would be good," I replied.

"What about next Thursday?" She sounded like she had just hit the lottery.

"Go ahead and book it."

"First-class?"

"It's the only way to go." I looked over at Lauren as she placed my sandwich with a Heineken on the table. I closed the phone and pulled the door shut. It was time for me to feed.

ABOUT THE AUTHOR

Born in Grenada, West Indies, Michael Presley migrated to the United States (Brooklyn, New York) in 1978. Upon graduation from George W. Wingate High School, he proceeded to get a Bachelor of Arts degree in English Literature at Stony Brook University. He has written various short stories, specializing in fiction. He is author of the bestselling *Blackfunk* trilogy. He continues to live in Brooklyn with his daughter and he is currently working on his fifth novel. Visit the author at www.blackfunk-book.com.

IF YOU ENJOYED "TEARS ON A SUNDAY AFTERNOON,"
BE SURE TO LOOK FOR

BLACKFUNK

BY MICHAEL PRESLEY

FUNK ONE

"Get the hell out," Andria screamed at the figure lying on the bed, naked except for a red condom on his penis. "Why the hell did you have to go and do that?" She stood holding on to the doorknob.

"I told you, Paul, I don't want this shit. I am twenty-six years old and I am tired of the games." A stream of tears flowed from her eyes down her face. "And—look at you—thirty-six years old and still doing the same old shit you use to do when you were twenty."

"Andria, can I explain?"

"Explain what?! Paul, there is no need for explanation. The picture is as clear as day."

"Don't we all make mistakes?" Paul leaned back on the headboard. He felt like a cigarette right now, even though he had recently given up smoking. "I never said I was perfect."

"You know what, Paul, just get the fuck out." She couldn't stop the rain from bathing her cheeks.

"Okay, I understand you're a little bit upset, but I want to come back when you have calmed down." He got off the bed.

"Who the hell do you think I am, Paul? Do you think you're gonna walk out and come back two hours later and everything will be okay?"

"Listen to me."

"Paul, get the fuck out before I stab your ass!" This time, she started to make her way toward the kitchen, her eyes red and bulging. This was not the life she had envisioned. Everything was all fucked up.

"Crazy bitch," Paul muttered under his breath as his eyes swept the room looking for his pants. He took a swipe at the rest of the colored condoms that lay on the night table. There were six remaining from the pack of a dozen he brought here two days ago. He turned and looked at her with a smirk on his face, not a hint of remorse. He had given her two years of his life, maybe not totally, but she was always his Number One. His body felt hot and sticky. He put his pants on without his underwear; he hadn't the faintest idea what Florence had done with it. And of course, now was not the right time to go looking for the fucking underwear. He had other things to worry about, including his love standing there, threatening to call the police. He was angry that she was telling him to leave. It may have been her apartment, but he was paying half the rent.

"Paul, I gave you everything! Why? Why? Look at me. There is nothing left to give."

"I'm sorry," he said as he looked at her and agreed with her statement.

He couldn't understand what went wrong. He thought he had played it safe. Andria was supposed to be at work until 5:00 p.m. He estimated it took her about one hour to get home. Florence had called him fifteen minutes after 11:00; she told him she was hot for him. The last time Florence was in heat, he had to wear an ice pack on his dick for hours, but it was worth every bit of that ice. He called Andria's job to make sure she was there. Mrs. Patterson, the short plump secretary on Andria's job, had said that Andria was in a meeting. City workers are always in meetings, meetings being one of the main reasons that there were few competent city agencies. He wondered how the city workers ever got anything done when they had this excessive amount of paperwork to muddle through and always had to attend meetings. He pressed the talk button on the phone and praised God that Mrs. Patterson's high-pitch voice was a distant memory. He hadn't given Andria her customary goodbye morning kiss because he heard her coughing last night. It didn't make any sense for them both to have a cold. Besides, she'd had that cold for over a week already, and it seemed to be getting worse. He hated colds. It made him feel like shit, though he didn't know exactly what shit felt like. He had told Andria that he wasn't going in today because he was feeling a little bit under the weather. He also had to fix the car to get it ready for their trip on Sunday. She knew his mechanic, a Jamaican immigrant named Rupert. Rupert was an excellent mechanic, but his rambling on and on made a simple ten-minute job take up to an hour. He told everyone who came to do repairs his life story, and boy did Rupert have a fucked up life story.

Paul actually did go to see Rupert. Rupert told him his car brakes needed a minor adjustment. Fifteen minutes later and twenty dollars poorer, Paul was back at his house relaxing, watching "Love Connection." It was after the show that Florence called. She was surprised to find him home, and she wanted to know if she could stop by on her way to the supermarket. She was going to bring Peter, her son, but she thought it might be better if she left him with her neighbor.

★★★

Paul had met Florence about a year ago when her husband had introduced his second half to him at a community meeting. He hated those community meetings but Andria had insisted that he attend. She told him he should get to know the people in the community that he was living in. Therefore, he did his usual, which was to sit in the back of the room and vote with the majority. To him, the most exciting thing about community meetings was the bored housewives. There were plenty of them tired of 365 days of that same old loving. Actually, depending on the marriage, sometimes there weren't even twenty days of loving in the year. There were all different kinds of marriages: arranged, prearranged, "you do your thing, I do mine," "let's stay together for the kids," "my husband is gay," or vice versa. America is a land of opportunities and sometimes if you don't do your job, another person will do it for you. Paul knew he took care of business at home, and occasionally, he was willing to help another brother take care of his shit. As soon as Andria introduced him to Florence, he knew the brother wasn't taking care of his business; therefore, Paul had to do the honorable thing. It was in her eyes. Her words were short and courteous, but her eyes were telling him about the quivering between her legs. Paul knew it, and Florence wasted no time in giving him her telephone number to discuss this new action committee. Andria was happy to see Paul showing an interest in the community.

Paul's interest in the community made her feel so proud, but now she knew why. She watched him as he stood up and put his clothes on. He was the gentlest and most loving man she had ever known. He knew how to make love to a woman. Their love making usually left her gasping for air. Even when he wasn't up to par, he used his hands and his mouth to open the sky for her, but most of all, she liked when he cradled her in his arms when they were finished. She liked the fact that he brought her flowers at least once every week. He would sometimes get down on his knees and clip her toenails. He would make dinner for her al least three times a week. And he would go with her shopping and not once would he complain, even when she went to ten different stores and left without buying anything. Paul was a good man. He made her feel safe and secure. In bed, he would do anything to please her, and obviously, he was willing to do the same for other women. Over the years, he had learned her body to the point that he could make her have orgasms at his will. Her friends had always been leery of him but they didn't know what she thought she had. She never told her friends about how good he was because she was afraid that they might want him. No, she didn't want to share him with anyone.

Florence had already flown through the door, hesitating only briefly to hoist her sleeping son over her shoulders. She knew the little boy should be getting up about now. Her girlfriend had told her that the pill she had given her son, crushed and mixed with juice, lasted approximately three hours. There were no side effects for the child. But Florence had seen her girlfriend's kids looking like they were doing everything in slow motion. She had wanted to ask Andria if she was going to tell her husband, but she thought better of it when she saw the look on Andria's face.

Paul stood six-feet-two inches tall. Two weeks ago, he weighed 230 pounds. Thick muscular thighs supported an ample stomach that hung over his genitals. He was a big man by anyone's standards yet he never tried to intimidate people with his size. He reached inside the brown dresser drawer and pulled out a rumpled gray shirt Andria had bought for him two years ago.

★★★

"Make sure you take everything, you fucking bastard, because I don't want to see your fucking face in my life again." Her face seemed contorted as if ice-cold water ran through her veins. She started to shiver, desperately wanting a blanket, but she didn't want him to see her break down. She had to be strong a little while longer.

"What do you want me to do, Andria? I said I was sorry and I am leaving! Okay?" He became agitated and as he looked at her, he wondered what would happen to them. The face that he enjoyed so much was now twisted in hate.

He remembered the time Andria brought him that shirt. It was about the same time they had pledged their undying love to each other, promising to talk to each other instead of talking to others. They felt it was important to leave the line of communication open because they knew other relationships where the couples did not talk to each other at all. They had seen how unhappy these people were, living in the same house but living two different lives. They both had had their share of meaningless sexual flings. They both talked about them openly, but he always got upset when she spoke of her past. He took that to be a man thing. He never wanted to admit that anyone had been there before him. He never wanted to believe that anyone had touched his sacred woman; she was going to be his wife one day. But he had gotten over that. He had come to realize that she had had a life before him, the same way he had had one before her. They had made plans to get married next year.

He was doing really well too, but then Cassandra from his job had invited him over to her place after work. He didn't plan to do anything even then, but that changed once he saw the ass on Cassandra. He wondered where she was hiding it before. God must have given her extra helpings. It started with her, and once the mold was broken, they started to pile up. After Cassandra came Joyce, Florence, Beverly, and Maria. He used a condom religiously with all the women; only once was there an accident. The condom broke while he and Cassandra were doing it doggy style. The following five weeks was hell until Cassandra got an abortion. She already had four kids; another one would bring her close to having a basketball team without a stadium for them to play in. Her husband was already raising one of her children from a man with whom she had had an affair.

Damn, he had a woman for every night of the week. Hell, this was the 90's and women outnumbered men five to one. And God knows enough of these men were fruitcakes so they didn't count. The women all knew Andria and they spoke very highly of her. Two were married with kids, and the other three were just beautiful, educated, horny black women. Maybe something was missing from their lives; but then that wasn't his problem.

Florence was a crazy bitch, but she was an excellent fuck. She could do things to a man's dick that would make his toes wiggle, and she was always willing to try anything new. Paul and Florence's husband played basketball in the park on Sundays. Florence would always be there, smiling at her husband as he ran down the court, and opening and closing her legs when Paul looked at her. Florence's husband told Paul that his wife was the best thing in the world. She was always cheering him on no matter what he was doing. Paul agreed with him down to her shaved pussy. Paul had told Florence that they had to cool it. Twice a week was getting too dangerous, and sometimes he had to do double duty. He wasn't twenty-one anymore, and she was starting to push the envelope. He once fucked Florence in her kitchen while her husband was upstairs sleeping. Paul had come over to pick him up to go to the park, and Florence had answered the door in a long tee shirt. She asked him if he wanted something to drink, and she guided him into the kitchen. There, she poured him a large glass of Tropicana orange juice, just the kind he liked.

A minute or so later, she bent over the kitchen table and slowly she lifted her tee shirt, exposing her beautiful curvaceous ass. He took a quick look upstairs and realized he was trembling. Florence slowly spread her legs apart; she took her hands and parted her ass. The Pope would have had trouble making a decision at that point. Paul had two choices. He saw the remaining used oil in the frying pan next to Florence's right hand. He touched it; it was warm. He dipped his hand in and slapped it between her butt. All she said was "oh." His penis had already saluted the entrance, something of a surprise considering he had just finished making love to Andria about a half-hour before. He was also taking chances with his life. The act was dangerous, and the risk out-weighed the pleasure. He should've turned away and walked out, but he knew it was too late. His other head was doing all the thinking. It was pussy power at its best. He was risking his life for a shot. Yet, he wasn't going to disrespect his woman by opting for the first hole. No, he had to go to the second. When he entered, Florence said thank you. He did not exactly finish the orange juice; neither did he wait for her husband to come downstairs to go play ball. After they had finished, Florence told him that her husband got a little bit too much for him to handle that morning. She smiled wickedly as the words left her mouth. However, she would be happy to go and wake him up after she had cleaned up. When Paul called her a "fucking bitch," she told him she would see him next week and he knew she would.

Damn Florence. She had to fuck things up. He tried to tell the bitch not to come over today, but trying to tell a woman, who is not thinking with her head, something logical, is impossible. He had concluded that a woman in heat was worse than a man. A woman in heat *had* to be fucked, and if her man wouldn't do it, she'd simply find someone else who would. Moreover, if that wasn't possible, electronic noise would sound or a cucumber would disappear from the refrigerator.

Paul wished Florence had found someone else today. As he continued to get dressed, he couldn't help but look at Andria. Florence had nothing on Andria. Andria was beautiful all over. She had short black hair cut so that it barely touched her ears. Her face had enviable brown skin with small, dark black eyes accented with full lips. There wasn't a blemish on her whole face. Oil of Olay should pay her millions for not using their products. Her walk was con-fident but with an undeniably sensuous sway. Her nose was small and straight. She stood five-feet seven inches with a shape that his friends compared to a

Coca-Cola bottle. It was her body that first attracted him, but the rest of her qualities he found out were even more precious than her body. He fell in love with her after six weeks of platonic dating. At that time, he didn't mind waiting for her because he still had a few booty calls from ex-girlfriends. He was so happy with her the first year they were together, but then things started to change. He could not put his finger on exactly what it was, but something changed. He used to bring flowers home to Andria every Friday. They would go to plays, movies, and sometime clubbing. He loved the way she danced. Then interest started to wane like it had with so many women before her, yet he tried to hold on because he knew she was special. He kept telling himself it was going to get better. It was at that time that he discovered that her beautiful body and nice personality were not enough. Many of his friends commented on her hint of pure sexuality, something he reveled in when he first met her. Her body was curved in all the right places, a slim body accentuated by a well-rounded butt. It was a model's body which he had the pleasure of molding in his imagination. Two years ago, he thought she was the most beautiful woman in the world; however, now, as he pulled his pants up, she was just another angry bitch. But God, what a sweet pussy! As he thought about her, he felt himself begin to rise. The condom dropped off into his pants and rolled all the way down his leg. He knew he had fucked up this time, but maybe she would let him eat first and fuck later. He looked into her eyes and realized the faster he got out of there, the healthier he would be.

"Help me, Lord! Help me, Jesus," Andria said as she walked out of the room. She was still reeling from what had just transpired. Her hands and knees still trembled. Only half an hour before, she had walked into the apartment and heard sounds coming from the bedroom. She wondered if Paul had left the TV on and the sounds were coming from a washed up soap opera queen. But as she reached the bedroom door, she heard the voices. It was unmistakably Paul and Florence.

"Come on, Baby; come on, do that shit," Paul encouraged Florence. "You are the fucking best."

Andria's hand had frozen on the silver plated entry lock. She wanted to scream but the words remained deep down in her throat. She felt herself gasping for air and sank to the floor, weakened by the thoughts that reality had brought forth. In the process, she had slightly opened the door.

"Fuck me! Fuck me," Florence's high-pitch voice squealed. Paul had seen

Andria fall down to the floor, but it was impossible to stop now. Florence was on top of him, her back to the door about to have an orgasm for the second time, and he was about to send millions of helpless sperm to their death inside a large, red condom. He looked at Andria as Florence continued her aerial stunts on his pole. He wished Andria would close the fucking door, join, do something. If not, the least she could do was wait until they were finished.

★★★

"No! No! No!" she whispered to herself, as she lay in front of the door. There was a pain deep inside of her throat, choking her. Her face felt wet and sticky. Her nose had stopped running and even that constant cough had disappeared. The world had suddenly stopped turning and she wanted to jump off. She mustered all her strength, pushed herself up off the floor, and ran to the kitchen.

"Mother fucking bastard!" Her mouth had begun to accept that salty tasting fluid coming from her eyes. She held on to the kitchen cabinet as she rummaged through the knife drawer. Fourteen inches of pure steel settled in her right hand, but she barely had the strength to hold on to it, and it fell to the floor. She pushed herself off the white Formica kitchen cabinet. The tears had stopped; now her face had become wrinkled and contorted. Her body shook, but she wasn't sure if it was due to symptoms of the cold or the present situation. Still, her course to the bedroom was set. Suddenly, she had thoughts of her mother coming to her room when she was six years old, a crazy thought because her mother was covered in blood. As quickly as the thoughts came, they vanished and Andria continued on her path to the room.

Now she lay slumped down onto the sofa in the living room. She had forgiven him once before. Even though she had never caught him, he had admitted to having an affair with Cassandra. Love had made a fool of her and now her heart was feeling the pain of believing in a fool's paradise. He had told her it was a mistake, and he promised it would never happen again. With tears in his eyes, he had asked her forgiveness and sworn on his mother's grave his undying love for her and his commitment to make her his wife one day. After that, he had shown her more love than she had ever felt from a man. He did everything she wanted and treated her like a queen.

For a long time after that, she didn't trust him. Their great sex life had become a battle of insecurities; her thoughts of him doing the same things and saying the same words to another woman became constant. She had lived a lie. She started to think about all the things they did together. Did he really go on a trip with the company? How many times did he actually stay at work to do overtime? Did Cassandra visit him at work? Did all her neighbors know, and had she become a big joke at dinnertime? They say once you do it the first time, the second and third time become easier and easier. How many women was he sleeping with?

She had gone to the doctor and taken every STD test that was available. Yet the doctor informed her that certain STD's had no immediate symptoms and some took a long time to show up. She made him take the tests too, and they both were clean. Now she had to go and do it all over again. How could he do that to her? How could he do that to someone he claimed he love? But time, the healer of all things, made life and love go on. In time, she forgave and in time, she learned to trust again. Maybe she had forgiven him because she never actually witnessed his infidelity. There is a saying, "a picture is worth a thousand words," but that wasn't true. This picture was worth a million words, and they were all flying around inside her head. And without a picture, the memory disappears with time. Now she had the pictures, videotaped in her eyes, forever etched in her memory to be eternally replayed. She now wondered how many other women he had brought to their bed, on his so-called days off. The questions kept pouring through her head. Each question raced the other for importance. How could she have been so gullible? Maybe he never had lunch during the day; maybe his lunch break had become a fuck break. Her anger and pain felt like daggers through her heart, slowly breaking it with deep wrenching pain. She felt used, betrayed, and put on stage to be the butt of a comic's jokes. Slowly, she was losing control. She needed to be away from here.

All her friends were either married or in relationships headed to the altar. She had invested three years in this man. She wanted a home with children, and she didn't want to go back into the dating game. The dating scene plagued with AIDS and all the other sexually transmitted diseases, had become a game of Russian roulette. Yet she didn't want to be alone. She realized now that home could be the most dangerous place of all.

"Why me? Why me? Haven't I been good, Lord?" The emptiness in the room let her echoed words match the space in her heart.

FUNK TWO

"Fuck you!" she screamed to the room. Her heart had become empty and heavy and the tears once again streamed down her cheeks, depositing their moisture into her gaping mouth. She again screamed, "Fuck you" to the empty room. The voice came from deep down in her heart and tore at her already tender throat. If it was exhaustion, she didn't know, but her mind had begun to drift to a better place…

Once more, thoughts of the incident at the age of six came to the forefront of her mind. Her mother had come into her room, bloodied and crying, pulled her into her arms, and steadily repeated, "I couldn't take it anymore. I couldn't take it anymore." Tears flowed freely down her mother's face onto hers. She kept asking what had happened, but her mother held her tight and kept rocking her. Then her aunt came in and pulled Andria away from her mother. Andria remembered screaming for her mother and fighting to get away from her aunt. Her aunt held on to her and carried her out of the house. As she sat in the car, the sirens bellowed in the distance quickly coming into view as police cars. Among the commotion of yelling men and crying women, her uncle emerged, lifted her up, and took her away. She did not get the news that her father was dead until a week later. She went to his funeral but couldn't see his face because the casket was closed. At that age, she did not know what death meant and for months, she waited for her father to return home. He never did and neither did Mommy.

Reality of the moment awoke her with a cough. She felt the mucous rising in her throat. Her face felt hot and her body was shivering. It was that nasty cold that made her leave work early today. Mr. Burke was very understanding. He saw that she was in no condition to work; he put her in a cab and sent her home. She resisted at first because she had some work she wanted to finish, but he insisted. Once in the cab, she realized Mr. Burke was right. She felt horrible. She couldn't wait to get home to seek the warmth of her bed. The Haitian cab driver, with his fake smile, gave her his home remedy for getting over colds. He told her to stop at the liquor store and pick up a pint of 100% proof Haitian rum; then told her she should mix some of that with honey and bula. The bula she should be able to get at any of the Chinese vegetable stores. She was amazed at the Chinese store. They supplied the black community with everything they needed except music. For a second, she thought about a Chinese rap group; it brought a smile to her face. Wherever there was a West Indian, there was a Chinese vegetable store. She thanked him and left him and his remedy in the cab. All she wanted to do was find her bed and slip under the covers. Unfortunately, her bed was already occupied.

★★★

Andria pushed herself off the couch and made her way to the armchair located at the edge of the carpet facing the Zenith 25-inch floor model TV. Somehow, the weakness she felt earlier had disappeared, but the lump in her throat constantly threatened her with nausea.

She dialed the numbers without feeling her fingers touch the phone, the same phone Paul had used earlier to make his plans.

"Hello?" the voice on the other line sounded tired and hoarse.

"Hello, Robin," Andria said, fighting the nausea that had begun to increase its upward flight.

"What's wrong, Andria?" Robin asked, immediately sensing the pain in Andria's voice.

"It's Paul, I…" Andria's voice trailed off to an unidentifiable whisper.

"Andria, what did Paul do to you? Did he hit you?"

"No, he did not hit me"

"What did he do?"

"In my own bed, he was doing it in my own bed."

"Andria, what are you talking about?"

"Robin, he and that fucking bitch were doing it in my own bed."

"Calm down, Andria. Everything will be all right. Now tell me what happened."

Robin listened to Andria tell her story, not once interrupting to ask any questions. Robin had known about Florence for a long time. When Andria was finished, Robin sat back, almost tipping her chair over in the process. She was a big girl these days, thanks to her husband's seed. Robin had told Andria to dump Paul when she found out that he had slept with Cassandra. She believed that once a dog, always a dog. She knew how well Andria treated Paul, and she knew Paul wasn't shit. Robin didn't believe in second and third chances. Once a person did something, the likelihood he or she would do it again was ninety-nine percent. Character flaws are hard to treat. They just keep coming back and back. She told Andria to cut him loose and move on, but now was not the time for "I told you so." Andria needed a friend to hold her hand. Robin was expecting this day to come eventually. She believed Paul was closer to dog-shit than an actual dog. But she also knew he made Andria happy, and she couldn't fight that. She believed that Andria should thank God she got out alive without catching AIDS or something. Robin told Andria she would come over and see her as soon as Jack, her husband, came home.

★★★

Andria took two swigs of the Russian vodka she had in the liquor cabinet and laid back on the brown antique couch in the dining room. At 6:30, a pounding awakened her. She shook her head back and forth to stop it, but it only got louder.

"Andria, Andria, open the door; it's me." The voice came from the direction of the front door. Andria took one step in the direction of the door, but her head started to spin and she fell back into her chair. The second time, she heaved herself up, and ignored the spinning in her head and swerving from side to side. She finally found the doorknob.

Robin's stomach pushed into the door, each breath trying to catch the other. These days her stomach was always the first to reach her destination. She was eight months pregnant. It was her first child, and each day she prayed for the delivery. She desperately wanted the baby, but the changes her body had gone through were driving her crazy. Robin had wanted a baby since she began having sex at fourteen. Her mother didn't find out she was sexually active until she was twenty years old. When she was in high school, her friends were having babies as if the summer season was dropping time. They would get pregnant in early September and have the baby in the early summer. Robin, herself, had a few close encounters with bringing life into this world. Once she had had a miscarriage, and then there was a false alarm. She wondered where the losers who had tried to make her a mother were today. As she grew older, she realized that having a baby involved more than making goo-goo eyes and rocking back and forth. It wasn't until Robin was twenty-eight and married that she got pregnant again. Now little Robin was kicking and turning inside her stomach.

Andria's hair was uncombed and seemed glued to her face. The remaining half of the cheap Russian vodka was nestled in the corner of the couch. Robin never knew Andria to drink any kind of liquor, much less vodka. Yet this time it was different. Andria was trying to chase that lump in her throat away. She was trying her best to exit a world that gave the illusion of a lifetime of happiness but only gave pain. No, Andria was hurting and Robin saw it in that haggled face without the assets of make-up to hide the lines. As Andria flopped back onto the sofa, her head rested against the sofa armrest with her right foot on the floor and her left foot completely on the sofa.

Robin headed to the kitchen to prepare another of Colombia's addictive exports. In a few minutes, the strong smell of coffee had replaced the stale aroma of the vodka.

"Sit back here and drink this," Robin said, trying to support Andria's head as she brought the coffee cup to her lips.

"No, I don't want that shit," Andria said as she tried to pull her head away from the ever-threatening cup of coffee. The curse word sounded strange coming from those perfect lips. "I just want to lay here and die," her voice said, rasping in its urgency and pain.

"Come on, Andria, drink this. Then we'll talk about how you're going to kill yourself. Remember that could be a very painful task, which would require sober thinking." Robin's faint attempt at humor did nothing for Andria's mood. She held the cup as Andria took the hot coffee in gulps.

Andria felt the constant throbbing etching out a pattern in her brain. She tried to rise, but the pain swimming in her head made it impossible. The most alcohol she had ever drunk was a small glass of cheap sweet Canei wine, and she had hated the taste of that too. However, this feeling was new to her, and her thoughts strayed to an old cliché "Mama never told me that love would hurt so much." With all the different functions going on in her head, one thought kept reoccurring to her. Why did he have to do this? She gave him everything she had. Is everything ever enough?

"The fucking bastard brought her into our bed. He didn't go to a hotel or anything," Andria said, trying to think of circumstances that would make the pain less. She knew this was the nineties, but these things didn't happen to her much less twice with the same person. "Granted, we haven't been having sex as often as when we first started seeing each other, but the passion was still there. We still had a lot of fun together, going places, doing things. What the fuck do men want, Robin?"

Robin wanted to say to Andria, "You knew this fucking two timing bastard was no good, so why are you acting like if he was some kind of saint." But instead she said, "I'm really sorry about what happened to you and Paul, but maybe it's all for the best." Paul was a player. He would fuck anything in a skirt. Robin had heard so many stories about who Paul was fucking that she stopped listening to them after they told her about Andria's next-door neighbor Phyllis. Phyllis was fat and ugly, two adjectives that should never be used to describe a person in the same sentence. If Andria only knew what Paul did, she would send him away with a bullet in his dick, kneel down, and praise God she was still alive. Robin did not tell Andria about Paul because she was afraid of losing a good friend. Besides, Andria would never believe her. Many friendships had ended like that. Andria also had forgiven Paul before for messing around on her; maybe she would have just forgiven him again. So had Robin told, who would be hurt the most? Still, Robin hated seeing Andria like this. Stress lines had taken up residency under Andria's eyes. Her face was a mask of confusion and anguish as she lay whimpering in Robin's arms below her extended stomach. Robin knew the phone calls would come much more regularly now, and she would have to spend countless hours telling Andria things that Andria already knew. But she didn't mind. She was happy to be there for her; she knew only time healed the wounds of the heart.

Andria's head lay in Robin's lap, as she slowly drifted in and out of sleep. Robin's legs had started to get stiff so she took a couch pillow and put it under Andria's head. Robin then got up and eased herself into the big brown leather TV chair, next to the couch where Andria was sleeping. Within ten minutes, she was in dreamland, walking on the beach with her family.

They must have slept for about five hours before the loud ringing of the phone woke them up. Robin saw Andria getting up, motioned her to lay back down, and went to answer the phone. She had looked at the stand for the cordless, but the handset wasn't there. She looked at the oval, off-white clock that hung against the wall, then at Andria. She felt she needed to spend more time with her friend. Her husband had gotten the note she had left on the refrigerator and wanted to know how she and Andria were doing. Andria was one of the few friends of Robin had that he actually liked. He asked her if she wanted him to come and pick her up. She told him to give her two more hours before coming.

Andria had finally gotten up and started attacking the dishes Paul and Florence had left in the kitchen. There were two plates with floral embroidery on them and two tall glasses from the Hard Rock cafe—the glasses they had received on Paul's birthday. Andria and he had gone to the cafe for dinner before going to see the Broadway play "Love Nest." That afternoon was completed with a carriage ride through the city. She must have spent over five hundred dollars that night, but she really didn't care. This was her man, who would one day be the father of her children; her life rotated around him like a carousel. As Andria washed each dish and glass with liquid soap, she threw them to the floor. The breaking plates brought Robin to the kitchen. She ran over to Andria and grabbed her hands; once again, tears flowed from Andria's eyes in an effortless stream. Andria threw her hands around Robin's neck as her body heaved and the pain returned.

Robin's hands circled Andria's waist from the sides and supported the three of them back to the room. Andria tried to apologize for her emotional outbursts, but Robin did not want to hear of it.

"Andria, you will get over him," Robin said as she guided her friend to her bed. She laid Andria down on the mattress and discreetly swiped a plastic condom wrapper from the edge of the bed, looking at Andria to see if she'd noticed. Andria's eyes were following Mr. Spock on a mission to another planet. Robin elevated Andrea's head with two pillows just in case the vodka got her a little bit restless. Andria muttered thanks to her and sank into a restless sleep.

Robin turned the channel on the small, cable-ready, digital, Sony 13-inch TV that rested on Andria's dresser. Channel 4 was showing the latest news headlines. The biggest story of the day seemed to be a woman claiming to have gotten AIDS from a date set up on the TV show "Blind Date." Robin shook her head and wondered; her mind became filled with questions of loyalty. Should she have told her friend about Paul and risked losing her friendship forever? Maybe she could have saved Andria from the sudden fall or worse, a painful death. Before she was able to justify herself to her conscience, Robin's thoughts were interrupted, by the loud ringing of the doorbell. She opened the door after her husband identified himself. She was relieved to see him and was happy because he was not Paul. She looked at Andria sleeping peacefully, but she knew that when she woke up the pain of consciousness would send her into misery. She kissed Andria goodbye and made a mental note to call her before she and her husband went to bed.

It was 11:30 that night when Robin, Andria's mother, the super, and the police opened Andria's door and found Andria's body bent over the toilet bowl. The right side of her face was lying across the toilet cover and her hands were dangling over the sides of the bowl. There were two tablets left in the bottle of Actifed. Upon seeing her daughter, Andria's mother began to wail. It was a loud eerie sound that echoed through the apartment, a mother's cry for her only child. Andria was her only good remembrance of a bad past. She had spent five years in prison on manslaughter charges. Andria's father was the only man she had ever had in her life. She held her daughter's hand tightly as the EMS technicians loaded her onto the ambulance. She prayed to God, asking Him to take her life but spare her daughter's.

The ambulance passed on Highway 16 with its siren blaring and Andria's mother holding onto her hand. The paramedics had revived her, and there was a weak pulse. If Andria's mother had looked out the window for a split second, she would have seen Paul's car parked in front of a two-car garage, attached to a house belonging to Joyce. Andria had also introduced Paul to Joyce and now Paul was about to enter Joyce's comfort zone. Andria had found notes that Joyce had left for Paul. They had a big argument over Joyce, one of the many promises Paul didn't keep. Actually, he stayed away from Joyce for two weeks before he started servicing her again. During that time, Joyce had met a cop with a very possessive personality, who claimed that she was his woman. She agreed with him; after all, she was approaching thirty, and it was time to settle down. But old friends with Paul's talent were very important to her and she needed some variety to add some spice to her life. Her man was always grunting as if he was doing something special, but he was only tickling her. Paul, on the other hand, made it be known that size does make a difference.

The doctor stopped pumping Andria's stomach at the hospital about the same time Paul stopped doing the backstroke. When they were finished, Paul told her his situation and Joyce told him hers. Two hours later, as Andria lay resting in her hospital bed, Paul pulled out of Joyce's driveway, and headed back to his forty-five dollar a night motel just off Linden Blvd. Tomorrow he would look for Cassandra. There are eight million stories in the naked city—this one was just beginning.